Last Call

Sydney Campbell

ISBN: 978-1-990231-21-6

Cover design by abu-chan
Editing by Megan Records

For my small (but growing!) amazing ARC team - thank you for taking this journey with me.

Other books by Sydney Campbell:

Allie Styles Romance
Temptation (Book 1)
Deception (Book 2)
Reckonings (Book 3)
Beginnings (Book 4)

The Allie Styles Romance Boxed Set

Courtyard Tales of Contemporary Romance
Reawakening (Book 1)
Redemption (Book 2)
Reckless (Book 3)

Mountain Valley Romance
Acting out of Love (Book 1)
No Reservations Required (Book 2)
A Dash of Romance (Book 3)
Coming Around Again (Book 4)
Last Call (Book 5)
Roadside Attraction (Book 6)
At Close Range (Book 7)

CHAPTER ONE

Bree

"Never in my life have I tasted anything so delicious. This is transcendent."

I smiled to myself as I turned back to my bottles, gearing up to mix the next drink. Jen cranked up the music, indicating that the last diners had left Cagney's restaurant for the night and all the action was focused on my turf: the bar.

I tied up my hair, ready to dig in and get serious. While the clientele at Adam Black's high-end restaurant kept me on my toes all shift, the end of the night was always rock and roll. In addition to the regulars, the tourists, and the late diners who migrated to the bar, I also had the kitchen staff to contend with—namely, Chef Liam and Sous-Chef Toni, two of my closest friends since moving to the small northern town of Mountain Valley.

The couple behind me were new customers and tasting my drinks for the first time. Being a small town, word had spread that people no longer ordered drinks at my bar—that I took a moment to assess them then mixed them the perfect cocktail. It was the reason a lot of patrons moved from their dinner table to the bar, eager to sample my wares for themselves.

Adam was thrilled, as I think I'd increased business three-fold since taking the job and moving to town. That had been about a year and a half earlier. I'd left my hometown of Vancouver after a bad break-up. Steve and I had been together for two years—the longest relationship I'd ever had. And then I'd walked in on him with another woman. Correction, my co-worker. It was enough to make me pack up and hightail it out of there, and off the west coast completely.

Everyone had thought I was nuts coming all the way up here, but it was the best decision I'd ever made. I felt like I was home. The friends I'd made were fantastic, I loved my work, and the best part of all? No one knew my history.

"Can I get another one of these?"

I turned back to the couple. The woman was smiling and holding up her glass. Bringing myself back into the moment, I took her glass and mixed her another cocktail, just in time for her date to hold out his. I repeated the process and moved down the bar, ready to take more orders.

Jack White was pumping through the speakers and I was in the zone. From the corner of my eye, I could see Liam and Adam watching me, talking in whispers. I knew the value I brought to the place, and I was glad they knew it, too. Adam was a gifted restaurateur, and Liam was hands-down the best chef I'd ever encountered, but if you didn't get alcohol in the drinking guests, what was the point?

Maggie Grant, Liam's girlfriend, slipped into one of the empty barstools and signalled for a drink. I smiled at her and mixed a gin and tonic. It had become Maggie's favourite drink, and sometimes a girl needs to stick to the standards. She smiled gratefully at me and took a sip.

"How's everything?" I asked.

I adored Maggie. She was a few years younger than I was, but wise beyond her years. A romance writer, she and Liam had hooked up a year earlier after a crazy ruse they had put on for her parents. They were the best couple and I loved watching their romance blossom right under my nose. We'd become pretty close over the past six months—two outsiders adjusting to life in Mountain Valley.

"Good. I'm just waiting for Liam to finish up. We're supposed to go away this weekend. First getaway we've had in ages," she said, a dreamy expression on her face.

"How's the writing going?" I asked, sliding over a bowl of mixed nuts.

"Pretty good. I just started outlining my third book. Second one is with the publisher now." She shook her head in wonder. "Some days, I still can't believe it."

"I can," I said. "Your writing is hot!"

She laughed and finished her drink just as Liam walked over.

"You ready?" he asked.

"You're not even staying for a drink?" I asked, feigning shock.

"Listen, I've got this woman to myself for three days. I'm not spending another second in this place. I'll see you on Tuesday," he said.

I leaned over the bar and gave Liam a kiss, then gave Maggie a quick one-armed hug. I watched them exit the restaurant, laughing with their arms around each other. I thought back on Steve for a moment and I may have placed the glass on the bar with a little more force than necessary.

Truth was, I really didn't care about *him* so much. I cared that he cheated on me. With another bartender. I had been seeking stability and security, two things I thought he was offering, but he'd just been having a mid-life crisis and was into bagging as many bartenders as he could.

I shook it off, grabbed a rag, and cleaned off the bar. I worked for a solid two more hours before the place finally shut down for the night. Exhausted, I grabbed my stuff and headed out, waving goodbye to Adam and Jen, the assistant manager, on my way.

*

The mid-July air hit me the minute I left the restaurant. While I can work up a nice sweat during my shift, the place is always air-conditioned and comfortable. The sticky July heat was like a shock to the system at quitting time during the summer months.

In winter, I drove to work, but in summer I couldn't resist walking. It didn't matter what time my shift ended; the streets of Mountain Valley were pretty safe. It was a small town and even though there were seasonal and weekend cottagers, everyone was friendly. It was another thing I loved about the place. It was a real community, something I'd been missing my entire life.

It was past two o'clock in the morning, but I wasn't surprised when I saw Lainey Wise coming around the corner with her dog, Bella. She lived pretty far out from town, but sometimes she and her boyfriend, Logan, would spend the night at the Anderson's B&B, which was about a kilometre up the road. Lainey was a screenwriter and loved her late-night walks almost as much as her late-afternoon naps.

"Fancy meeting you here," I said, feeling cheesy the moment the words were out of my mouth.

"How you doin'?" she responded in her best Joey Tribiani voice, making me laugh out loud.

"I'm good. Just off shift, heading home. You?"

"Ignoring the fact I have an early call tomorrow."

"Oh, shit," I said. "That's right. You're on set for your film, right? How's that going?"

Lainey ended up in Mountain Valley, where she'd been born and raised, after a seventeen-year absence because she was working on a film for Mason Scott's production company, which had set up shop in town. Mason had opened the studio after being here on a location shoot and falling in love with Katie Simon, the owner of the local bakery.

"Pretty boring. I mean, I'm sure it's interesting for the cast and crew, but me? I basically sit around all day working on other projects until someone has some changes to discuss. Please remind me never to do this again. I like writing the movies, not filming them."

I laughed, thinking how many people would die to be in her position. But I got her point. I'd been on a couple of sets and knew exactly what she was talking about. A lot of hurry up and wait. At least it gave her some cash while she and Logan set up their home together. High school sweethearts, they'd just reunited after an almost two-decade separation and it was safe to say things were going well with them.

We walked together for a bit, as my apartment was on the way back to the B&B. There were several creative housing options in a small town like this, and I had opted for one of the less traditional ones. An enterprising hipster had bought a huge old house, gutted it, and renovated it, essentially turning it into two separate houses, one on each floor. I had the top, and Nick Felton lived on the bottom. He was out of town for a bit, so it was like I had the place to myself. It was heaven.

I let myself in, climbed the steps, and went straight to bed. It had been a long day.

CHAPTER TWO

Dave

It was ten to ten when I turned the key in the lock of MVP, or Mountain Valley Phono, the record shop I'd owned for the past five years. My dad had laughed when I'd bet him I'd become a business owner by the age of thirty, and I'd pulled it off just in time, at twenty-nine. Granted, it wasn't the business I *thought* I'd be running, but I had no complaints.

I wasn't late that morning, but I was cutting it close. Not like it really mattered. On a gorgeous summer day in Mountain Valley, no one was coming in to shop for records.

It was the kind of day that demanded to be spent outdoors. Whether hiking, hanging out at the public beach, or enjoying the spoils of private lake access that came with owning or renting a cottage, it was definitely an outdoor day.

Jed, the previous owner of MVP, had warned him of the double-edged sword of summer. It was the season with the most potential for revenue, due to the influx of tourists and seasonal renters, but it was also the time people were least interested in record shopping.

I walked in and turned on the lights, then bent to pick up the mail. Walking down the aisle towards the counter along the sidewall, I stopped every couple of steps to adjust albums left askew by previous browsers. I walked behind the cash, dropping my bag, and flipped on the stereo system. Selecting something from my private stash was the way I got into work mode each morning, and I took great care in how I set the day's mood.

I pulled Jethro Tull's *Aqualung* off the shelf and slipped it onto the turntable. Music on, I turned to the day's mail. The first couple were bills, but the third was a notice. The building had been sold, a new developer was taking over, and rents were being increased.

What the fuck? Didn't news like this usually come by registered mail?

The record shop was surviving, but that was it. There was no way I'd be able to handle a rent increase. Before I had a chance to sink my teeth into the problem, the door opened and Katie Simon walked in. She flashed me a huge smile and made her way over.

"Hey, Dave, how's everything?" she asked.

"Um, great. Things are great." I shoved the letter under the counter and gave her my best smile.

She squinted at me, then cocked her head to the side.

"Not sure you and I have the same definition of great. Want to talk about it?"

"Nothing to talk about. What can I do for you today? Rare of you to be out of the bakery at this time."

Katie and her two partners, Jax and Tess, ran Franni's Bakery, Mountain Valley's best spot for baked goods, cakes, and all the town's catering needs. Because aside from being a wizard with butter, sugar, and flour, Katie knew how to cook. Thanks to her, I didn't starve most days.

"I'm shopping for Mason's birthday. I was thinking of putting together a few albums that mean a lot to us," she said.

"How romantic of you," I said, smiling. "What did you have in mind?"

We spent the next thirty minutes going through the shop while she selected her albums. It was a great collection and Mason would be thrilled. One of Hollywood's hottest leading men, he'd planted roots in Mountain Valley after falling in love with Katie while filming here on location. I'd gotten to know him a little, and he was a cool guy. I was happy to help her out with this.

I walked back up to the cash to ring her out, and she just stood there, staring at me.

"What is it, Katie?" I asked.

"There's something off. Come for a drink with me tonight. Let's hang out. We haven't done that in ages."

It was true. We hadn't. In fact, it had been a long time since I'd hung out with anyone. I usually hibernated through much of the winter, coming out only to open and close the shop, and I still hadn't really gotten back into the swing of things yet.

"What did you have in mind?"

"Cagney's?" she suggested. I snorted.

"Maybe something a little less trendy." I countered.

"Hey, have you been there yet?"

I shook my head. Zero interest. I liked the classics, the mainstays. I had no desire to check out every new joint that opened up in town. Most of them shut down again within the year.

"Then you shouldn't judge. It's not trendy. The food is outstanding, and they have the best bar in town. Yes, before you say it, better than Elena's."

"I doubt that," I mumbled.

"It's settled. I'll be back here at six to pick you up. We're going for a drink. I might even convince you to have dinner with Mason and me."

I laughed.

"I doubt it, but I'll agree to the drink."

She smiled, grabbed her tote bag filled with records, and walked out.

*

At six on the dot, Katie breezed back into the shop with an expectant grin on her face. I rolled my eyes and closed up the cash, grabbing my keys and meeting her at the door.

"I can't believe you talked me into this," I said.

"I didn't. It was never a discussion."

I laughed, appreciating her tactics.

"Where's your boyfriend?" I asked.

"He's meeting me at seven, which gives me exactly an hour to convince you to join us for dinner."

"Katie. What's going on? Am I your new project or something?"

She stopped in her tracks and looked at me.

"Hey. Not fair. We're friends. And I haven't spent time with you in ages."

"Okay, okay."

We continued walking towards the restaurant in silence for a bit.

"Plus, I could tell you'd gotten bad news or something this morning," she muttered under her breath.

"Oh, for fuck's sake."

"Don't be mad at me. You don't have to talk about it. Let's just have a drink and enjoy each other's company."

I smiled despite my annoyance.

"That I can do."

We rounded the corner and ended up in Cagney's parking lot. Katie led the way, opening the front door and motioning me inside. I walked in and it was pretty much what I expected—nice tables, atmospheric lighting, art on the walls. But the mood was different than I'd thought. Instead of being stiff and reserved, people were loud, laughing and having fun. There was none of the pretentiousness I'd been so sure I'd find.

Katie walked up to the woman at the maître d' stand by the door. They exchanged a quick hug and I spotted a discreet name tag that read "Jen." They chatted for a moment and Jen pointed to two empty seats at the bar. Katie smiled and grabbed my hand, leading me over.

"So? Is it as terrible as you thought?" she teased.

"Actually, no. It seems pretty cool. My mistake."

She grinned ear to ear and I had to laugh. We took our seats and Katie had a quick look around, I guess trying to see if Mason had arrived early. Behind the bar, the bartender stood with her back towards us. She was dressed in black jeans, a black tank-top, and had jet-black hair that fell down her back, spilling across her bare shoulders but revealing a small tattoo of the moon on her left shoulder.

"Bree!" Katie called out, startling me so much I jumped a little.

The bartender turned around and I felt like I'd been punched in the gut. There was no air to be had. I swallowed a few times, trying to find my voice as they exchanged greetings and Katie introduced me. I managed a small smile.

"Hey," I said.

"Hey, yourself," she laughed and turned back to Katie.

I tried to pull my eyes away, but it was nearly impossible. I'd never had this kind of reaction to another human being and I couldn't figure out what the hell was going on. My fucking heart was racing.

"I'll, uh, have a scotch," I said, completely interrupting their conversation.

Katie glanced over at me, a curious look on her face. I drank beer. I had no idea what made me order a scotch. I felt an unfortunate heat spreading across the back of my neck. I swallowed again. *Get a hold of yourself, man.*

"How about I make you a cocktail?" Bree asked.

"Uh—"

"It's kind of what she does," Katie offered. "She's really good at it. Go ahead, Bree. I have no idea what's gotten into Dave."

Bree turned and started pulling down bottles. Katie turned to me so fast I was surprised she didn't develop whiplash.

"What is wrong with you? Scotch? Since when do you drink scotch? And why are you staring at her like that? What's going on?"

"Nothing is going on."

"Do you two know each other?" she pressed.

"No."

"So why are you blushing like the two of you just made out in the back alley?"

"Can you drop this?" I asked.

Bree turned around and deposited two drinks in front of us. I smiled and picked up my glass, taking a sip. I coughed, choked, and sputtered.

"Are you okay?" Katie asked, rubbing my back.

"Yeah, fine," I said, once recovered. "I hate gin. I'm sorry."

Bree stared at me, blinking.

"Really?" she asked.

"Really," I said.

"Shit, I'm sorry. That's never happened before. What do you want?"

"How about a beer?"

She nodded and pulled out a pint glass, filling it from the tap and handing it over.

"On me," she said, smiling as she turned away.

CHAPTER THREE

Bree

It was a busy night, and I kept my focus on the work, but every now and again, I'd glance over at Katie and her friend, puzzled. *He didn't like gin?* I'd never read a customer wrong before. I'd certainly never had a drink returned. Was I off? Or was my ego just bruised?

I'd never seen the guy before. Dave, Katie had said his name was. A bit awkward, but in my line of work I saw it all. He looked like he was a few years older than I was, dressed in jeans and a concert T-shirt. He was the only other person in the place in jeans besides me. He was cute, but his hair was way too long. I shook my head as I mixed the next drink. Never understood that type. Clean-cut was where it's at.

I brought them another round of drinks: Bree special for Katie, another beer for Dave. What the hell did he do for a living that he dressed like that coming from work? I'd never met him on the bar scene, so I doubted he was a musician. Probably some ski bum living in his mother's basement. But he didn't look like a ski bum. He was completely devoid of that bro attitude I despised so much. This dude looked like a cross between a philosophy major and a biker.

"Get your pass for the festival?" Katie asked when I came over to wipe down the bar.

"I did. Can't wait," I said.

She was referring to the Mountain Valley Rock Festival, an annual music extravaganza that blew through town every August. I'd missed last year's, as it was my first summer and I was just settling in, but nothing would stop me from seeing this year's lineup. Some of the best in indie and alternative rock, with a few big names for headliners.

"That must bring you good business," Katie said, turning to Dave.

Ah.

Dave shrugged.

"It does. Especially if some of the performing acts come by for signings," he said, glancing up at me.

I took the bait.

"What do you do?" I asked, sliding the bowl of nuts towards him.

"I own MVP, the vinyl shop?"

I stopped and considered him. It fit. But I was impressed regardless. I nodded and turned to serve some other customers.

By the time I got back to them, Katie was gone and it was just Dave finishing off his beer.

"I take it Mason showed up?" I asked.

Dave looked up at me, startled, then seeming to recover, nodded quickly. He pointed his chin towards one section of the restaurant and I looked over and saw the lovebirds laughing over the menu. I smiled. I adored seeing them together.

It seemed like over the past year everyone I knew was coupling up. Katie started the whole thing when she met Mason, and it was like she'd infected the entire town with some kind of love bug. People who had never committed before were now in serious relationships. First my boss, Adam, and his girlfriend, Tess. Then Chef Liam, the original bad boy, and Maggie. Even Lainey and Logan had managed to find each other, after seventeen years apart, right here in Mountain Valley. It was starting to make me a little nauseated.

I looked back at Dave. He had a weird look on his face, like he was trying to sort through something in his head, having a whole internal dialogue and everything.

"You okay?" I asked.

Again, he started. He looked at me and smiled nervously.

"Yeah, just a rough day."

Now that was more my territory.

"Wanna talk about it?" I asked, putting out a fresh coaster and another pint of beer.

He sighed.

"Let me guess," I said. "Broken heart."

He raised one shoulder, then let it drop.

"I guess?"

"You're real talkative, aren't you?" I laughed.

Suddenly, he looked up and glanced down the bar. Then he turned his attention to me.

"You ever date clients?" he asked.

"Aha," I said. "I'm beginning to see where we're going. Yes. Of course, I do. Where else would I meet people?"

"So imagine everyone at this bar were single. Which one is most your type?"

I was surprised at the question, suddenly unsure where he was heading, but I took my time and looked around. Jeff Patterson, a regular, was standing at the other end of the bar with some colleagues. He was around forty-five, married with kids, but he was cute and relatively fit. He was in a light grey suit, powder blue shirt underneath. No tie. *Rawr*.

I discreetly pointed with my chin.

"That one."

Dave casually glanced over and nodded subtly.

"Why?" I asked.

"Just curious," he said.

I studied him, trying to figure him out. He was a tough read, which was rare for me. I still couldn't believe he didn't like gin.

"Let me make you another drink," I offered. "Give me a chance to restore my reputation."

He smiled, slid off his stool, took a fifty out of his wallet, and left it on the bar.

"Maybe next time," he said, then walked out of the restaurant.

*

A little before ten, Tess came in to wait for Adam to finish up. She grabbed a seat at the end of the bar and I poured her a nightcap. The two of them worked so hard it was crazy, and I was always happy to do whatever I could to make their days a little brighter.

She smiled her thanks as she accepted the drink, then took a long sip. She closed her eyes and sighed.

"Long day?" I asked.

She rolled her eyes.

"A new developer is buying up property around town. We're fine, before you say anything. Katie owns the building Franni's is in. But it's not good."

"How is this guy buying up everything?" I asked.

"Not everything. Specific properties. Old Man Cromway died in debt, so his properties went up for auction."

"How do you know all this?" I asked, eyeing her with fascination. The woman worked relentlessly—when did she have time for gossip?

"Everyone was talking about it today. Apparently, those affected got letters in the mail. Can you believe it?"

Tess shook her head and took another sip, downing her drink. She gave me a sheepish look. I took her glass and poured her another. She smiled gratefully.

I left her to serve a customer, but I thought back to Dave and his forlorn expression. I tried to think if Cromway had owned the building his store was in, but I really hadn't lived in Mountain Valley long enough to know all the finer details. I grabbed my rag and headed back over to Tess.

"Hey, Tess? You know that guy, Dave? Owns MVP?"

Tess looked from her phone and gave a rueful laugh.

"Yeah, I know him. I even tried to hook up with him one winter. Good thing that didn't work out."

Without glancing up, I kept wiping down the bar.

"Oh yeah? Why's that? He an ass?"

"Not at all. Great guy. Quiet, but super smart and funny when you get to know him. Nah. Wasn't that at all. He was just a shit kisser."

"Really?" I asked, looking up. "That bad?"

"That bad," she confirmed. "Why? You interested? Doesn't seem your type."

"No, no. Nothing like that. I was just wondering—you know what? Never mind."

I turned and walked down the bar, taking off my apron to get a fresh one. What was I doing? What the hell did I care about this guy and his potential rent problems? Wasn't like me to think about a customer after they'd left. It must've been my inability to read him, to mix him the perfect drink. Bastard had gotten under my skin.

CHAPTER FOUR
Dave

By the time I got home, the sun was setting and there were tinges of pink and red going through the sky above the lake. The record shop wasn't the only thing Jed had sold me. His cottage on the lake had been part of the package, and he'd been so anxious to get out that we'd worked out an interest-free private loan that made me feel like I'd hit the jackpot.

I didn't even go inside but walked around back and down to the dock, where I sat in my favourite chair and looked out over the lake, waiting for darkness to settle over me. I closed my eyes and within minutes heard the familiar summer sound of the bullfrog's mating call. I smiled to myself and got up. I went into the house, grabbed a beer from the fridge, and went back out to enjoy the concert.

It took about 3.5 seconds for my mind to drift back to the notice. Jed had advised me years ago to buy the damn building MVP was in, but paying off the shop itself plus the house was more than enough debt, thank you very much. Now I was starting to see his point. He'd been really fucking smart, and I should've listened to him.

I had no desire to leave Mountain Valley. Ever. But I couldn't fool myself into thinking this new arrangement would be viable for me. The shop was already struggling and jacking the rent up wasn't just going to be another expense, it was going to sink the business. And a small town wasn't exactly brimming with career possibilities.

I took a swig of beer and listened to the frogs. They had it all figured out. Life was pretty simple if you were a frog. Eat, swim, mate—what else was there to do?

I peeled the label from the bottle, an easy task given the night's humidity. The bartender. I shook my head, smiling at the thought of her face when I choked on the drink. Her disbelief when I told her I hated gin.

I loved gin. But I realized within thirty seconds of meeting her I'd never have a shot, and I needed to stand out. What better way to do that than by getting under her skin? She was famous across town for her uncanny ability to match drinks to customers. She wouldn't forget me so quickly.

The cocktail itself had been fucking fantastic.

I tried to remember the last time I'd reacted that way to a woman. From the moment I saw her face, I was struck. I knew all about instant attraction and lust, but this was something entirely different. Just thinking about her caused a weird sensation in my gut.

It was going to be a long night.

*

First thing the next morning, I was on the phone with the bank. Of course, I wasn't the only one calling. From what I'd heard, this developer had bought up all of Cromway's properties and jacked up all the rents equally.

The bank manager wasn't very encouraging. Apparently, since Cromway hadn't raised our rents in years, the new owner was just bringing everyone up to market value. He promised to review my file and we set an appointment for the following week.

I hung up the phone just as the first customers of the day walked into the shop. It was a group of teenagers, summer renters. I flashed a smile. They were often my best customers, bored kids of wealthy parents who had money to burn. It was just my luck that vinyl had made a comeback.

I'd never thought of myself as a salesperson. A music lover, yes, a salesperson, not really. People came into the shop and we talked about music, then they bought some records. There was no pressure involved, just a shared love of a common art form. I never even thought of what I did as work. I got to ruminate on my favourite subject every day. What could be better?

I'd never be rich, and I hadn't spent four years in college to run a record shop, but somewhere along the way, I'd decided that quality of life was more important than money. It was a decision I'd never regretted.

Until now.

I glanced up at the kids, who were still browsing, and asked if they were looking for something in particular.

"You got any Pearl Jam?" one kid asked, eyes hopeful.

"Sure thing, dude. Let me show you."

I walked over and showed him what I had, then turned to help one of his friends. We chatted about shows and the upcoming festival in August, and by the time they left an hour later, they'd dropped two hundred bucks between the four of them.

Maybe I could learn to be a salesperson.

*

At six, I locked up the shop and headed for my car. It had been a pretty good day overall, and I was feeling optimistic about things. Well, as optimistic as I got. I had planned to pick up some Thai food and go straight home but somehow found myself driving towards Cagney's. I couldn't get the damn woman out of my head.

I parked in the lot and considered calling someone to come meet me. I hadn't given the whole thing much thought and suddenly I was uncharacteristically nervous about going in alone. And I went everywhere alone. Restaurants, movies, festivals—it was the only way I was able to get some peace and quiet to process everything.

I was being a fucking chicken. I pulled the keys from the ignition, got out of the car, and walked into the restaurant. I was greeted by Jen and told her I just wanted a seat at the bar. She smiled kindly and pointed me towards an empty spot.

I sat down, enjoying Jackson Browne playing on the sound system. I'd just been reading the history behind *Doctor My Eyes* that afternoon and it seemed highly coincidental to hear the song playing. I waited silently until Bree turned and caught my eye. She threw me a warm smile and walked over.

"Hey, Dave, right?"

I nodded.

"You want to order or do you want to give me a chance to redeem myself?" she asked.

Bingo.

"Is that important to you?" I asked.

"It's important to my ego," she laughed.

"Go ahead, then," I said.

I watched as she pulled down a few bottles, mixed a drink, and poured it over ice. She turned and placed it on the bar with a confident smile.

I picked up the glass and took a tentative sip. It was fucking delicious. Like, out of this world. I wrinkled up my nose and put down the glass.

"A little too sweet for me," I said.

"Fuck me." She pulled a mug out from the freezer, filled it with draft beer, and slid it across the bar. I took it with a smile.

"What is it with you?" she asked. "I never get this wrong."

I just shrugged and drank my beer.

"Hey, Bree, can I get a refill?"

Bree turned around and I followed her gaze to a guy at the other end of the bar. It was Owen Bates, the manager of one of the three big banks in town. I'd met him once or twice through Jed. He was probably close to fifty. He was a decent guy but dull as wood.

Bree flashed him a brilliant smile and made her way over to him. I couldn't hear them over the noise, but they chatted for quite a while. I noted with irritation that he made her laugh a few times. Not the kind of laughter that reached her eyes, but still.

I downed the rest of my beer and held up my mug. She nodded at me and walked back to give me a refill. She then served a few other customers before returning to me with a bowl of nuts.

"Sorry. Forgot about these," she said.

I reached for a handful. Popping them in my mouth, I nodded towards Owen.

"He's been watching you," I said.

"Oh, I know. He'll be asking me out before closing."

"I'm sure you've got a standard rejection," I said, laughing.

She looked at me, curious.

"Why would I say no?"

I stopped laughing. I glanced over at Owen in his navy suit, black hair cut close to his scalp, goddamn pocket square in his jacket. Then I looked back at Bree, a woman who vibrated with life. I shook my head.

"Sorry. I guess that was out of line."

She sighed.

"Listen, he's a nice guy. Got a great job. I'd be more than happy to go out with him."

Now or never.

"And if I asked you out?"

It was her turn to laugh.

"I like you, Dave. I do. But you are most definitely not my type."

She turned to serve another customer, leaving me feeling once again like I'd been punched in the gut.

CHAPTER FIVE

Bree

It was a busy night, but Owen found plenty of time to flirt. He was cute and he'd been after me for a while. I just knew this was going to be the night he took the plunge. Sure enough, by the time I brought him his third round, he asked if I was free for lunch the next day.

A lunch date. That was sweet. I smiled and cleared his empty glass.

"That sounds lovely, Owen. I'd love that."

He grinned and we made a date for the next afternoon, somewhere close to the bank I'd never been to. I gave him my best smile as he paid his tab and left. I looked down after he was gone. He'd left a decent tip. This might work out.

I hummed to myself as I made my way down the bar but stopped when I caught Dave's eye. He was smiling, but it was a sad smile. I walked over and took his empty glass.

"You want another?" I asked.

He shook his head.

"No, thanks."

"On me," I offered.

Again, he shook his head.

I put my elbows on the bar and leaned in towards him.

"Everything okay, Dave?"

He gave me a quick smile but said nothing. He was a quiet one. I was used to guys who didn't shut up. This was completely outside my realm of experience. I tried again.

"Everyone's been talking about this new developer in town, and how he's jacking up all the rents. You caught up in that?"

A pained look crossed his face. It was brief, but I saw it. *Bingo.*

"Yeah. It really fucking sucks," he said.

I reached over and took his hand.

"I'm sorry. That's gotta be rough. I know a few people affected. Is there nothing you can do?"

"Nothing but come up with the money."

He said nothing more, and neither did I. What more could I say? I felt bad for the guy. I liked him. He was quiet but quirky. And I could tell he was smart.

"You're a clever guy. I'm sure you'll figure something out. Your shop is part of this town's DNA."

"Says the woman who's never set foot in the store."

"Ouch!" I laughed. "It's not like I've been around that long."

He nodded slowly.

"What's it been? A year? A year and a half?"

Busted.

"I've got a Spotify account," I admitted.

His hand flew to his heart like he'd been wounded. I laughed again.

"Oh, Bree. I'm so sorry you don't experience music the way it's meant to be experienced."

"I've survived this long," I said.

He shook his head, giving me a sad look and sighing. I couldn't help but smile. He nodded towards the end of the bar.

"Bates left," he said. "I should have bet you."

"You'd have lost. I'm having lunch with him tomorrow."

Dave raised one eyebrow and smiled.

"I guess women really do know."

"This one does."

*

My alarm went off at ten the next morning. I despised setting an alarm. It was one of the perks of working nights—I got to sleep in as late as I wanted. But then I remembered why the alarm had gone off and I rolled out of bed.

I drew the curtain, letting the July sunlight in through the window. It was a gorgeous day. I went to my dresser and was about to pull out a pair of black jeans and a tank-top, then had a change of heart. I opened my closet and found my black, boat-neck sheath dress. It was classy but casual. I brought it with me into the bathroom, figuring the steam from my shower would get rid of any wrinkles.

By the time I was dressed and ready to go, it was close to eleven-thirty. I grabbed my bag, slipped on a pair of flats, and made my way to the restaurant.

There were three banks in town, and each one of them had an upscale restaurant next door. It was an ingenious move, knowing there'd be clients to impress and not many options in the area. I liked Mozart, the place I was meeting Owen, and there were a few more dishes I was eager to try on their menu.

By the time I got there, Owen was seated at an outdoor table, nursing a drink. He got up and smiled as I approached and I leaned in for a kiss on the cheek before taking my seat.

"You look beautiful," he said.

"Thank you." I smiled, reaching for my menu.

He said nothing as I studied the options, but I could feel his eyes on me and a blush started to creep up my neck. That was unlike me. I was not a blusher. But his blatant attention was making me a little uneasy. I flashed him a nervous smile as I put down the menu.

"What are you having?" I asked.

He flashed me a wicked smile.

"For lunch?" he asked.

Oh, shit.

"Because for lunch I'm having the goat cheese salad, but I was hoping that maybe later—" he leaned across the table and whispered in my ear.

I shot out of the chair so fast my water glass tipped over, spilling its contents across the table. I didn't make a move to clean it up. I stared at Owen. OWEN!

He was still grinning wickedly. I shook my head.

"I think you misunderstood something," I started.

He shrugged his shoulders. I gathered my things and turned to leave. Then I turned back.

"You know, you came across as a really nice guy."

Again, he shrugged.

"Maybe you don't read people as well as you thought."

He laughed at his perceived cleverness, and the sound of it echoed in my head long after I left the restaurant.

*

Heading back home to crawl into bed, I passed the bookstore and realized I hadn't been in in a long while. I was pretty sure Mrs. Fairfax, the owner, had also been hit by the increase and could do with the business. I could certainly do with a new book. And the idea of losing myself in another world was pretty tempting at the moment. One that didn't contain creeps like Owen Bates.

I walked in and was instantly greeted with a smile. Mrs. Fairfax came out from behind the counter to give me a huge hug, making me feel even worse about how long I'd been gone.

"If it isn't Bree Rollings," she said. "What brings you by?"

"I'm so sorry, Mrs. F. Really. I've been so busy with work and it's been a long time since I've read a good book."

"Well, you've read Maggie's, right?"

I smiled.

"Of course." Maggie's debut had turned into a bestseller. It had taken a little while, but word of mouth sent that book up the list and she'd become pretty hot property.

"What did you have in mind?"

"Not sure. Maybe I'll just browse a bit." I looked around. "Shane working today?"

Mrs. Fairfax dropped her gaze for a moment before meeting my eye again.

"Actually, I had to let him go. Only way I could manage the rent increase."

"Oh, Mrs. F., I'm so sorry."

I leaned in and gave her another hug, resting my head on her shoulder for a moment.

"You should come into the bar one night for a drink. I mix a mean cocktail, you know that?"

She laughed with delight.

"So I've heard. But cocktails and bars at night aren't my speed anymore, love. Why don't you go browse?"

I nodded and walked through the store. It was hard to imagine someone like Mrs. Fairfax managing the entire place on her own. Shane had been working there for years. I turned back to the cash.

"Has Shane found other work?" I asked.

She smiled.

"Right away. He picked up a job at the library. It was his major, library studies."

I nodded, pleased. At least it had worked out for him. I still couldn't help feeling bad for Mrs. Fairfax, though.

I wandered the rows of fiction, running my finger along the spines, stopping every once in a while to read the blurbs on the back. I took a few from the shelf and walked towards the cash.

Mrs. Fairfax went through them and smiled.

"This is a nice selection, love. Will you have time to read all these?"

"I'll make the time." I pulled out my wallet. "Listen, you sure you're okay with all this space? Maybe you can downsize the shop or something?"

"Don't you worry about me, love. I'll work it out."

She rang up my books and I pulled a reusable bag from my purse. I packed up my purchases, gave Mrs. Fairfax another quick hug, and left the shop.

I turned left to head home, then had another flash, and turned right instead. I paused for a second, wondering if maybe I should just stay out of the whole business altogether. But then I shook it off and walked down the street, determined.

CHAPTER SIX

Dave

It was close to one and my stomach was growling like crazy. I was thinking about closing up the shop and heading across the street to the diner to pick up a burger. It was the first time in a while I'd forgotten to bring lunch and I was starting to dream about a good, greasy cheeseburger.

Mind made up, I stepped out from behind the cash just as someone walked in the front door. Irritated, I glanced up and was shocked as all hell to see Bree standing there, paper bag in hand and sheepish grin on her face. She was wearing this black dress thing and she looked hot as hell.

"I figured it was time to check out the record shop."

I had about three point five seconds to figure out how I was going to play this.

"What you got there?" I asked, nodding towards the bag.

"Lunch?"

I nodded slowly.

"I thought you had a lunch date with Owen."

Her eyes widened and she hurried down the aisle towards me and whispered in a conspiratorial tone, "Turns out Owen's not such a nice guy."

If I had hackles, they'd have gone up.

"What did he do?" I asked, keeping my tone even.

She leaned over and whispered something so dirty in my ear I blushed. I stepped back.

"He said that to you?"

She nodded, trying to contain her glee.

"What did you do?" I asked.

"I stood up and walked out. What the fuck do you think I did?"

She opened the bag and pulled out two deli sandwiches, two bags of fries, and two soft drinks. Neither was diet. I smiled and reached for a sandwich.

"I gotta ask you, Bree. Why the suits?"

She shook her head.

"Way too personal. This friendship is just beginning."

She jumped up on the counter and smiled at me, unwrapping her sandwich. It was like the goddamn sun came out right in the middle of the fucking record store. Friendship. That's what she was offering. I could do that.

I walked back behind the cash and pulled out Van Morrison's *Astral Weeks*, slipping it onto the turntable and dropping the needle. A smile spread across Bree's face as she pulled a fry from the bag and popped it in her mouth.

"This is the magic you were referring to?" she asked.

"I don't believe I ever used the word magic," I answered.

"Semantics. I knew what you meant."

I sat on my stool and picked up my sandwich, considering it before taking a bite. For a moment I thought about lying and telling her I didn't eat smoked meat, but I felt like I'd already won that battle. She was here. I took a bite and contained the groan of ecstasy that wanted so badly to escape.

She looked around the store as she ate and motioned with her hand towards the front section, which was filled with all the requisite crap every record store carried.

"You've got a lot of wasted space here," she said. "Does that shit even sell?"

I looked at the paraphernalia and shrugged.

"The posters do. Not much of the other stuff," I admitted.

"Then get rid of it."

"Hey, I thought you were here for a friendly lunch."

"Sorry." She smiled. "I am. Let's eat."

I glanced at the other bag she'd been carrying.

"Been shopping?" I asked.

"Yup. Picked up a few books at the bookshop. I hadn't been in ages. It was great to see Mrs. Fairfax."

"I love that woman," I said. "One of my greatest pleasures is browsing in that shop."

She smiled and nodded in agreement. Just then, the door opened and a group of teenagers came in. I put down the sandwich and watched them for a few minutes, fully aware that Bree was studying me, head cocked and a curious smile on her face. I glanced over at her.

"What?"

"You look like me, assessing a customer. You reading them?"

I gave her an enigmatic smile and walked over to the group. One of them had been in a few times and I knew he'd be a good customer. I appreciated him bringing in his friends. I clapped him on the shoulder.

"Hey, Glenn. Good to see you. These your buddies?"

Glenn nodded and introduced me around. I looked at one guy, a redhead, and took in his Zeppelin concert T-shirt.

"You heard the debut Greta Van Fleet album?" I asked him.

"Who's that?" he asked.

"Oh, my word," I answered, and proceed to pull the album out of its sleeve as I walked back to the turntable. I took off the Van Morrison record and replaced it with *Anthem of the Peaceful Army* and waited.

Two chords into the first track, the kid was hooked. I turned to the next kid and we started talking about Prince. The entire time, I was aware of Bree's eyes on me. Why had she come? She'd been clear I wasn't her type, so it appeared she really did want to form some kind of friendship. I glanced back at her and she smiled as she considered another French fry.

By the time I finished with the kids, she was done her lunch and had hopped off the counter, dusting crumbs from her dress.

"I should let you get back to work," she said.

"Thanks for coming by," I said. "Really. This was great. I was starving."

"Huh. Look at that. I finally got something right with you."

She threw me a smile over her shoulder as she walked out the door.

*

I closed the shop an hour early, hanging a sign on the door with my apologies. It had been slow since four and I desperately needed to talk to someone about all this shit that was going on. I figured I'd go by the bakery and see Katie. At the same time, I could pick up some dinner and, well, who was I kidding? A little dessert.

When I got there, Katie was nowhere to be seen. Neither was Tess. In fact, the only two in the shop were Jax and Chance, which was weird because both of them usually stayed in the kitchen. They were both up front clearing out the shelves.

"Hey, Katie around?" I asked.

"Hello to you, too," Jax said dryly.

"Sorry. You're right. Hey Jax. Chance. How you guys doing?"

"Just fucking peachy," Jax muttered. "And no, Katie isn't around. Can I help?"

"Didn't you hire someone? Why are you guys—" I started.

"Didn't work out," Jax said, cutting me off. "Again, can I help?"

He put down the tray he was holding and gave me his full attention.

"Actually, you can. I've got a bit of a problem."

Jax put up his hand.

"Stop right there. I'm tired of being therapy guy. Not in the mood tonight. A blond-haired, blue-eyed god broke my heart last night and I just don't have it in me."

"Dude. I'm sorry. Do you want to talk about it?"

Chance started shaking his head slowly in terror behind Jax's back. But Jax just sighed sadly.

"No, that's okay. That's what my colleagues are for." He looked me up and down. "And you don't have any colleagues. Tell you what. You can borrow Chance. I'm going to clean the range."

Jax sauntered into the kitchen, leaving Chance and me to stare awkwardly at each other. I knew the guy and we were friendly, but it wasn't on the same level as my relationships with the other three. There was probably no reason for that besides time spent, but he was not my go-to for this. In a small town, word spread quickly and I need to be careful who I confided in. In fact, Jax would've been a terrible choice. I resolved to wait for Katie.

"Just let Katie know I dropped by. Tell her to come see me tomorrow if she can," I said.

"Sure thing," Chance said. "Positive there's nothing I can do for you?"

"Actually, there is. What's the dinner special tonight? And have you got any cheesecake left?"

CHAPTER SEVEN

Bree

Saturday night was insane. The restaurant was packed with a waiting list and the bar was overflowing—standing room only. I'd called in reinforcements and Jen was working with me while Adam took over hosting duties. I loved when she joined me. We had the best time together, pumping the music up loud and turning our bar into the best party in town.

Owen made an appearance. I'd told the staff the story and Jen offered to serve him but I waved her off. I was nothing if not used to unwanted advances—even the extremely obscene ones. I was still so shocked, though. He'd seemed so vanilla.

Every once in a while I found myself scanning the crowd for Dave. I hadn't spoken to him in a few days, since I'd gone by with lunch. We were similar, and I could certainly do with a few more friends in town. It hadn't been hard uprooting to move here, but that didn't mean making friends had been a snap.

I'd been blessed with great colleagues and their partners, who turned into friends, but I had little outside of work that was mine. Dave was smart and funny and I saw the opportunity to widen my circle. Also, he was one of the few guys in a long time who hadn't made a pass at me, so at least I knew there were no romantic interests involved. Thank God. I kept thinking back to what Tess said about his kissing and it made me shudder.

He didn't come in, but every time I did a scan, I noticed Liam and Adam chatting in the corner. There were a lot of glances in my direction and by the end of the evening, I was starting to get a little suspicious. They'd clearly been talking about me and I was eager to know what it was all about.

As the place emptied, the staff came out of the kitchen and gathered around the bar. It was tradition, especially on the weekends, to close out the night with a drink or four. I left Jen to pour the shots and took a seat next to Liam. He smiled and threw an arm around me. I leaned my head on his shoulder.

"I saw you guys tonight. What's going on?" I whispered.

A lazy grin crept across his face. Chef Liam, with his huge, tattooed arms and close-cropped hair, was smoking hot—and he knew it. He was also the most devoted boyfriend I'd ever seen, following Maggie around with a puppy-dog look in his eyes at all times. Watching the two of them get together last summer had been a staff-wide event, each of us betting when they'd hook up first. Well, hook up for real.

"Don't flirt with me, Chef. Just tell me what's up."

He shrugged and handed me a shot before downing his own.

"I'm going to wait for the boss," he said, wiping his mouth with the back of his hand.

"Someone talking about me?"

I turned around and saw Adam, our boss, standing behind us, also wearing a shit-eating grin.

"What is up with you two?" I asked.

Adam thrust his hands in his pockets and rolled up onto the balls of his feet.

"We're putting together a new tasting menu," he said.

"Okay. What's the big news about that? You do that once a month. Get me the menu and I'll pair the drinks," I said, reaching for another shot.

"Well, that's the thing," Liam said, smirking. "We need your input first."

I almost choked.

"Excuse me?" I asked.

"We're going to put together a tasting menu based around your cocktails. A tapas-type thing. But Liam and I thought it would be fun to turn it around and base the food on the alcohol."

That shit-eating grin was contagious. I couldn't stop smiling. *This* was the fucking recognition I wanted.

"How does that sound?" Liam asked.

"That sounds fucking fantastic," I said.

I laughed and called to Jen for another round of shots.

*

Sunday morning was just painful. I may have stayed too late at work, and I most definitely drank too much. I held my head as I rolled over and said a little prayer of thanks for Nick's extended trip. If he'd been home, there'd have been music coming up from the first floor at a very undesirable volume.

I felt around on my night table, where I'd had the foresight to put a bottle of aspirin and a glass of water. I took a few pills, drank some water, and pulled the covers back up over my head. I figured I'd sleep for at least another few hours.

Then I remembered the menu, and a smile broke out across my face. Then I remembered Jen saying she'd fill in for me that day and the smile turned into a slight giggle. I rolled over, closed my eyes, and drifted off into blissful sleep.

*

When I woke a few hours later, I stretched luxuriously for about ten minutes before getting out of bed. I stumbled to the bathroom and showered, then had a quick breakfast over the sink. Surveying the fridge and pantries, I decided it would be a good idea to get groceries.

While I normally went to the supermarket, there was a general store I loved shopping at when I had the time. Which wasn't often. It had been ages since I'd had two consecutive days off in a row, and with the restaurant being closed on Mondays, that was exactly what I was getting. It felt like I had all the time in the world.

I pulled out what I lovingly referred to as my grandma cart and made my way to the store. I saw a few familiar faces along the way and stopped to chat. I was still a newcomer by Mountain Valley standards. Sometimes it felt like it would be years before they considered me a local, but it didn't bother me that much. I was patient.

By the time I made it to the store, I'd worked up an appetite. I bought a ridiculous amount of food, along with a baguette, an apple cake, a focaccia pizza, and a pint of ice cream.

I made my way from the bakery to the produce section, grinning as the memory of the menu popped into my head again.

"What so funny? The pears particularly amusing today?"

I looked up at the familiar voice and saw Dave holding a cantaloupe. I smiled.

"Wait," he said. "Don't move."

I was holding a grapefruit and a bunch of bananas. I cocked my head.

"It's just that I've never seen you with so much colour," he explained, breaking into a grin.

I laughed and dropped the stuff in my cart before making my way over to hug him hello.

He gave me a one-armed hug but squeezed my shoulder in this way that felt like he was really connecting. It was nice.

"How you been?" I asked, eyeing his cart.

He glanced down at the assortment of healthy foods in his cart and gave me a challenging look.

"You've got something to say about my groceries?" he asked, glancing into my cart.

"Not a thing. I'm walking around with carb central here. I applaud your restraint," I said.

He shrugged.

"I like this shit, believe it or not. It's what I was raised on. Didn't your folks feed you healthy food growing up?"

I felt the storm pass through my eyes as he said it, and I knew he saw it because he grew very still. I said nothing.

"Sorry," he said. "None of my business what you ate growing up. Come, let's hit the butcher."

I smiled gratefully and we pushed our carts towards the meat counter.

"Hey," I said. "What are you doing here on a Sunday? Aren't you working?"

"Nope. Store's closed on Sundays. I need a day off," he said.

"And you chose Sunday? That seems stupid. I'd think the weekends would be busy."

"Listen, I need a day off, and if I take it during the week, I'll spend it running errands. Groceries are the only thing I do on Sunday. It's fine."

"What about a part-time employee?" I asked.

He paused.

"To be honest, I'd thought about it. But that rent hike pretty much obliterated that idea."

It made me think of what Mrs. Fairfax had said about having to let Shane go. This asshole was really fucking with a lot of my friends.

"So what do you do with the rest of your day off?" I asked, changing the subject.

"Absolutely nothing."

I smiled.

"Why don't you come over? We'll hang out. I've got the day off, too. We can make some food and watch some movies."

He held up his hand as the butcher came over to take his order.

"I'll have two rib-eye steaks, a pound of old-fashioned smoked meat, and two of those filet skewers in the corner."

The butcher nodded and got to work. Dave turned back to me.

"I'm in for the movies, but how about we order the food?"

I laughed.

"What about the food you just ordered?" I asked.

"That's for the week. Today's my day off. Don't you listen to a word I say, woman?"

I rolled my eyes at him and we made our way to the cash. I'd invited him over on impulse, but I was glad I had. The more time I spent with Dave, the more I liked him. And it had been a long time since I'd hung out and binged movies. It was shaping up to be a great day.

CHAPTER EIGHT
Dave

Had it been as simple as telling her I hated gin? Because for the life of me, I couldn't figure out why Bree had taken to me so quickly. It was clear she had no romantic interest, but she also didn't hide the fact she enjoyed spending time with me.

I wasn't complaining.

We parted ways outside the general store after she gave me her address. I told her I'd drop my shit off at home and head over to her place.

"You sure you don't just want to stash your stuff in my fridge?" she asked.

"Positive. Besides, I will not be seen walking through the streets of Mountain Valley with that thing," I said, indicating her ridiculous shopping cart.

She hugged the damn thing defensively and pouted.

"Don't mock my cart," she said. "It serves me well."

I grinned as I walked to my car, unable to believe my luck. I drove home, dropped off my groceries, and on a whim, grabbed a gram of weed and some rolling papers. I followed the directions to her place, which was on the opposite side of town.

I pulled over to park outside the address and recognized the house as Nick Felton's place. I'd been there once before, shortly after he'd moved in. He'd had a house party, but that was long before Bree had shown up in town.

She was waiting for me out front. She'd changed into a pair of denim shorts and a white T-shirt, and her hair was pulled up in a ponytail. I'd never seen her in anything but black before and she looked amazing.

"Hey," I said as I approached.

She smiled and opened the door for me. I followed her up the stairs to her place, which was laid out exactly like Nick's but decorated with a lot more style.

"Nice place," I said.

"Thank you."

I followed her into the living room and she dropped onto the couch, passing me the remote.

"You choose," she said.

I raised my eyebrows as I took the remote.

"Me?"

"Yup. It's a test. To see if I can hang out with you or not."

"No pressure," I mumbled, sitting on the couch beside her.

She didn't scoot over, which I took as a good sign. I hadn't sat uncomfortably close, but if she'd wanted distance between us, she wasn't showing it. I flipped through the onscreen menu, making a conscious decision to choose something I liked, not something to impress her.

"Have you ever seen *The Bridges of Madison County?*" I asked.

"Of course," she laughed.

"Have you ever seen it high?" I held up my baggie of weed.

A smile broke out across her face.

"Why no, I haven't. Why don't you twist one up? Let's do this."

She grabbed a blanket from an open crate by the side of the couch and threw it over herself as I used the coffee table to roll a joint. She hit play on the movie just as I lit up and passed it to her. She took the joint from me, then passed me some of the blanket, which I pulled up over my lap as I settled back against the couch beside her.

We spent the first twenty minutes of the film passing that joint back and forth, and every time her fingers brushed mine, a bolt of electricity shot up my arm. I couldn't understand how she wasn't feeling it, too. When we finished smoking, her entire body relaxed and she melted into my side. It took all my restraint not to put an arm around her, but I did pull the blanket up a little further as she lay her head on my shoulder.

The first time Meryl Streep and Clint Eastwood got together, she let out a little sigh.

"I'd forgotten how good this movie is. I'm surprised you're such a romantic."

"Why is that so surprising?" I asked.

She shrugged against me and I could feel every inch where our bodies were touching.

"Look at me. I run a record shop, I wear jeans and concert T-shirts, and my hair belongs in the seventies. Of course I'm a romantic."

She looked up at me and smiled, then turned her attention back to the movie. I froze when I caught her first sniffle. I hadn't really planned for crying. Soon enough, her shoulder was shaking slightly against me. I had no choice. I pulled my arm out from under the blanket and wrapped it around her shoulder. She threw an arm lazily across my abdomen and for a second, I thought my heart had stopped.

I didn't know her well, but I knew she wasn't a tease. This was just how she was with her guy friends. Affectionate. That was cool. I had plenty of friends like that. This was no different. I focused on the movie and got lost in the plot for the next half hour.

By the time the credits rolled, I'd joined her in the tear fest. She looked up at me and laughed.

"You're laughing at me?" I asked.

"You're crying."

"Yes, I am. I'm exposing my soft underbelly and you're laughing. Nice."

She reached up and stroked my cheek, wiping away a tear with her thumb. I fought to keep my eyes open.

"You're right. I'm sorry." She paused for a moment. "Have you got any more weed?"

I freed my arm and untangled myself from the blanket. She scrolled for another movie to watch while I rolled another joint. I passed it to her and she lit it, smoking quietly for a moment before passing it to me.

"I don't have a family," she said.

I looked at her.

"You mean you've disowned them?" I asked.

She shook her head and took the joint from my hand.

"I mean, I don't have a family. My parents died in a car accident when I was one."

"Oh, Bree. Shit. I'm so sorry."

Again she shook her head.

"They had saved up all their money to take a road trip, a little break...a babymoon, I think it's called. Anyway, they were driving at night and collided with an 18-wheeler truck. The driver had fallen asleep at the wheel. All three died instantly."

I reached over and took her hand.

"My grandmother, who'd been watching me, raised me for the next few years. But then she got too old and had to move into a home, so with no other family, I was put into foster care. I was very young and very angry, and that made me very unadoptable.

"I bounced around from foster home to foster home until I hit eighteen. Then they set me loose." She gave a mean laugh. "I met this woman, probably in her twenties, who came in to talk to us sometimes. She was a writer. She'd also grown up in the system and made it a point to talk to young women about shaping their futures. I took that to heart. I got my act together, got a job, put myself through school, and graduated with a degree in psychology."

"Bree."

I wanted to say more, but she didn't seem quite finished, so I shut my mouth. She put the joint down in the ashtray and got up from the couch. She walked across the room and turned to me, smiling sheepishly.

"You'd once asked me why the suits."

Ah.

"I've had to take care of myself my entire life. I'm fucking tired, Dave. You know? I've worked hard, I've got a great job, great friends, but there's never been anyone to look after me. That's why the suits. Those guys are men. They're in their forties, they're established, they've got money and a desire to take care of another human being."

She laughed, more to herself than anything else.

"Sure, the sex is often kind of vanilla, but that's a pretty small price to pay in the grand scheme of things, don't you think?"

"No."

She looked at me, startled.

"Excuse me?"

"I'm sorry. I just mean I don't think you should settle for a type of guy who you think will take care of you. You deserve better than that. You deserve earth-shattering love."

She smiled sadly.

"I thought so, too. And I thought I had it. Until I got home one day and found my fiancé sleeping with my co-worker."

"Oh, fuck. Bree, I'm sorry."

"Stop fucking apologizing to me."

"Right. So— Right."

"Anyway, that's how I ended up here. I ran. It's easy to run when you're not leaving anything behind."

She plopped back down on the couch next to me and retrieved the joint, relighting it before taking a long drag.

"Thank you," I said quietly. "For confiding in me."

She smiled such a sweet smile my heart constricted.

"You're easy to talk to. Easy to be with. I like you, Dave. I hope we can hang out more."

"Anytime. But, I gotta ask you. A bartender with a psych degree?"

She shrugged and passed me the remains of the joint.

"I tended bar to put myself through college, but I ended up loving it so much I kept it up. And the degree just helped me read my customers better. They say bartenders are like therapists. At least I'm qualified. And I'm saving my clients a fortune in fees."

She laughed as she picked up the remote and hit play.

"My turn," she said. "*Goodfellas.*"

CHAPTER NINE

Bree

It was past midnight by the time Dave left. I felt awful, knowing he had to work the next day, but we'd both lost track of time. At some point in the evening, we'd paused our movie marathon to order dinner and were both pleasantly surprised to learn we loved the same pizza toppings. We watched four movies together, with me getting the final choice. We agreed to call it a night and pick it up again another time.

As I watched him walk down the front path, I smiled to myself. He was such a great guy. I wondered why he didn't have a girlfriend and mentally went through my contact list to see if I had any single friends I could hook him up with. I came up empty and decided to keep an eye on the female customers at the bar for a change. There was no reason for this guy to be single.

After his car pulled away, I went back inside and tidied up before heading to bed. It was almost decadent that I still had another day off, and I drifted off to sleep easily after a day well spent.

*

Monday was all about the usual day-off things, like laundry and running errands. One of those errands included the bank, which was right by Franni's. I popped in for a quick hello and a dozen croissants.

"Bree!" Jax shouted when I walked in the door.

He crossed the floor in three strides and pulled me into a bear hug. Jax and I had bonded as soon as I'd moved to town, both of us enjoying a fun night out. He used to go bar hopping with Tess, but once she and Adam settled down together, she kind of lost that party streak. I was more than happy to fill the void. Jax was a great dancer.

I pulled away and gave him a kiss on each cheek. He tousled my hair and stepped back, studying me.

"You look different," he said.

"I'm relaxed. This is my second day off. IN A ROW."

He burst out laughing and then just as quickly the smile vanished from his face.

"I remember those days," he said wistfully.

"Aw, does being a partner mean putting in the real hours?" I teased.

He and Tess had been brought on as partners by Katie, who inherited the bakery from her grandmother. The three of them were an unstoppable team and they were in talks for franchising the business. From what I understood, Katie wasn't keen, but she was open to the idea of a second location in LA. She was spending a lot of time there these days.

"Pretty shitty what's going on with the rent hike, huh?" I asked.

"Yeah," Jax agreed. "Thank God Katie owns the building."

"Seriously. I was talking to Mrs. Fairfax the other day. She had to let Shane go. And then Dave and I were talking and —"

"Dave Winter?"

"Yeah, why?"

"I don't know. I've never heard you mention his name before."

"We just met," I said. "He came into the bar with Katie the other day. Nice guy."

A sly smile crept across Jax's face.

"Don't get any ideas," I said. "He's not my type."

"Oh, I realize. He doesn't wear a tie. Probably doesn't even know what a pocket square is."

"Jax."

"Besides, he hasn't acquired that dad bod yet..."

"JAX!"

Jax just laughed and tousled my hair again. No one tousled my hair. Well, no one but Jax. For some reason, it didn't bother me when he did it. But if anyone else tried, they'd lose their fucking hand.

"I'm just teasing you, Bree. He's a great guy. And I can see the two of you being friends. You're a lot alike in some ways."

I smiled at that.

"Hey! Did I tell you what Adam and Liam dropped on me the other night?"

Jax shook his head and I told him about the upcoming tasting menu. He freaked out as a good friend should, and then promised to round up the staff for dinner when the menu launched. I paid for my croissant, gave him a hug goodbye, then left to finish my errands.

My last stop, the dry cleaner, brought me within half a block of the record shop. I hesitated for less than a second before heading over to say hello. There were a surprising number of people milling about, but Dave caught my eye as soon as I stepped in and threw me a smile.

Not being in any particular hurry, I browsed while he served his customers. Naturally, I checked to see if he stocked all my favourites. I wondered if that was the standard operating procedure for anyone walking into a record shop, the desire to know if one's tastes were deemed worthy of owning on vinyl.

It was a good forty-five minutes before everyone cleared out. Dave made his way over to me, grinning.

"Couldn't keep away, huh?" he asked.

"Yeah, that's it. I just wanted to make sure you'd recovered from your crying jag. Those first ten minutes of *Up* were pretty rough on you," I countered.

"Those first ten minutes are rough on anyone with a heart."

"Ouch!" I cried, bringing my hands to my chest.

"Whatcha got?" he asked, nodding towards the box from Franni's.

I smiled and set it down on the counter, opening it to reveal the heavenly croissants within. He grinned and reached in to grab one. He practically moaned as he took a bite.

"Seemed pretty busy in here," I said.

"Yeah," he said between mouthfuls. "Summer can be kind at times. I take advantage when I can."

"Hey, listen. Jen called this morning with the schedule. I'm off at eight on Wednesday. Want to hang out? We can fit in a couple of flicks before midnight."

"Sure," he said. "Sounds great. I'll come by the restaurant after I close up and wait for you."

He was standing behind the counter across from me, nothing but the cardboard box between us. He took another bite of his croissant and a piece of flaky pastry clung to his upper lip. I smiled and he looked at me, curious. I reached over and brushed the crumb away with my thumb and he took my wrist.

Neither of us moved. We both stared at each other, frozen in our action, suspended in the moment. I could've sworn I heard both our hearts beating in unison. Finally, he let out a laugh and released my wrist, letting my hand drop and wiping his mouth with his forearm.

What the hell just happened?

I looked into the box, taking my time selecting a croissant as I tried to recover from whatever the fuck that had been. I had never felt a moment of discomfort with Dave, and while I wouldn't have classified that exchange as uncomfortable, it certainly wasn't in line with the easy camaraderie we'd established. When I was finally brave enough to look up at him, I found his gaze trained on me, an unreadable expression on his face.

I closed up the box and pushed it aside.

"Great. Maybe you'll let me mix you a drink."

"You're still stuck on that?" he asked, laughing.

"My ego is fragile," I said.

The moment had passed, and I was grateful.

CHAPTER TEN

Dave

On Wednesday night I closed the shop with a spring in my fucking step. I wasn't an idiot. I was getting nowhere with her, but just the fact that I was spending so much time with Bree lately was enough to keep me in a permanent state of contentedness. And that was despite the fact I was about to lose my business. The woman was good for my soul.

I got to the restaurant at the height of the dinner rush, but at Bree's request, Jen had saved a seat for me at the bar. That felt fucking special. I caught her eye as I got onto the barstool and she came right over with a beer. I raised my eyebrow.

"You're not even going to try?" I asked.

She had a very guilty look on her face and I was instantly on guard. I looked around but saw nothing out of the ordinary. Chef Liam was at the other end of the bar, but that wasn't anything unusual.

"What's up?" I asked.

"I have to cancel," she said.

"Oh. Everything okay?"

"Yeah. It's not that. It's just, well, I got asked out."

I did my best to maintain a neutral expression as my heart dropped into my fucking gut.

"Oh. Okay. Which one?" I asked.

She cocked her head without turning around.

"Dark grey suit, white shirt."

I glanced down the bar and sure enough, there was a guy, around forty-five, in a suit and sporting a close-cropped haircut. He was clean-shaven and drinking scotch.

"Looks like quite a catch," I said.

"Right? That's why I want to go fishing. Are you mad? We'll do it Monday, I promise."

What the fuck could I say?

"Of course I'm not mad. Monday would be great."

She leaned over the bar and gave me a quick kiss on the cheek.

"Thanks, I owe you."

She took off her apron as she walked to the end of the bar. She grabbed her purse and sweater, gave Jen a high-five as they swapped shifts, and took the suit's arm as they left the restaurant together. I let out the breath I didn't realize I'd been holding.

"You like her."

I stiffened, turning to see Liam sliding onto the empty stool next to me.

"What makes you say that?" I asked.

"It's okay, dude. It's cool. I like you. You'd be good for her." Liam reached for the bowl of nuts and grabbed a handful.

"Moot point," I mumbled. "She's got no interest in me."

"Of course she doesn't. You're under fifty and wear jeans and concert T-shirts."

I laughed.

"You noticed that, too, did you?"

"Listen," Liam said, leaning in. "I love Bree like a fucking sister, but she's got ass taste in men. I don't know what she thinks she's looking for, but it ain't that."

"Have you ever told her that?" I asked.

"Have you ever tried telling Bree anything?" he countered.

"Fair enough."

"She talks about you all the time," Liam said.

That surprised me.

"Really?"

He nodded.

"Yeah, but not like she's into you. I think you're too far in the friend zone, man. I mean, she likes you, you got that going for you, but it'll be a long road to get her to *like* you, if you know what I mean."

"Yeah, I know what you mean."

He studied me.

"You're really hurting."

"Is it that obvious?"

"Fuck, yeah. Have you tried telling her?"

I shook my head.

"No. I don't want to mess this up. I fell for her the first second I saw her, and every minute I spend with her is a gift. If this is all I get, it's all I get. I can live with that."

"No you can't, man. You might think you can, but you can't. You're selling yourself short. You just need to find a way to show her she's barking up the wrong tree with those suits."

I turned to him.

"She will never go for me. I can't offer her the life or security she's looking for. I'm about to lose my damn business. You think she wants to deal with that?"

"Shit. Sorry." He grabbed another handful of nuts. "Listen, we don't know each other that well, but like I said, you're a good guy. I'm rooting for you."

With that, he got up from his stool and went back into the kitchen.

*

The text came in around midnight.

Maybe a movie would've been better.

I smiled. I felt bad, but if her date had sucked, I was thrilled.

Was it Owen-level bad?

No! Jake was a perfect gentleman. We had a lovely time. I'm going to see him again next week.

Suddenly I wished I had ignored my phone.

So why would a movie have been better?

There was a slight pause. Then the three dots, then nothing. I waited.

We went for dinner, and dude, I had the pasta and it did *not* sit well.

Great. Jake the Suit gets to date Bree and I get to hear about her upset stomach. I was rapidly attaining best friend status but somehow felt like the loser. Even though I knew Jake would be gone within weeks, if not days. Had he kissed her? *Fuck.*

Sorry to hear. Listen, I'm beat. Chat tomorrow?

Yeah. Have a good night.

I put down my phone and rolled onto my back, staring up at the bedroom ceiling. Had Liam been right? Was it time for me to talk to her, tell her how I felt? I tried to imagine every possible scenario, every outcome, but each time I played it out, it ended badly.

But there'd been that moment in the shop over the box of croissants. I hadn't imagined it. Something had passed between us and she had felt it. I just had to figure out how to make that happen again.

CHAPTER ELEVEN

Bree

Dave texted me on Monday afternoon, inviting me to his place instead of returning to mine. I was curious to see where he lived, so we made a plan to meet there at seven. I was in charge of picking up dinner.

We hadn't really spoken since the previous Wednesday and I had a feeling my getting dinner was supposed to be some kind of restitution for standing him up. I felt bad about it, but he'd seemed okay at the time. And friends understood that kind of shit. Guys like Jake didn't come along every day. He was kind, gentle, and had a great job.

The week had gone by quickly. I'd been testing out cocktails on customers each night and while I'd noticed that Dave hadn't been by, I hadn't really had the time to check in with him. When the weekend hit all hell and broke loose—I'm not sure I even slept between Thursday and Sunday. By the time Monday came around, I was exhausted. I slept most of the day, getting up late in the afternoon to shower and get ready.

When I pulled up outside Dave's place, I let out a low whistle. It was a gorgeous cottage nestled into the woods, right on a small, non-motorized lake. There was a kayak moving through the water as I got out of my car and approached the front door.

Before I had a chance to knock, the door swung open and Dave stood there. He was dressed in a pair of jeans, no shirt, no socks, and his damp hair fell around his shoulders. He was holding yet another concert T-shirt in his hand. I was momentarily caught off guard. Where had those abs come from? And tattoos? Holy shit.

"Hey," he said, smiling, pulling on his shirt.

"Uh, hey. We're never going to my place again. This is fucking paradise."

He laughed, delighted, and ushered me inside.

"What did you bring?" he asked.

"Sushi. That okay?"

He nodded and took the bag from my hand. I followed him through the open-plan living/dining/kitchen area where he placed the food on the counter. The house was amazing. Huge, airy, exposed beams everywhere. Comfy furniture and a fireplace. A real cottage. There was even a pair of antlers mounted on the wall.

"This place is amazing," I said. "I know I'm gushing, but Jesus, Dave."

"I know. I bought it off Jed. Package deal with the record shop. It was honestly the best part."

"No kidding."

He started unpacking the food and I looked around for plates and glasses. We met up at the table and sat down to eat. We didn't say much, but it was a comfortable silence. I finally asked him about his day and we got into a long debate over that stupid merch wall again.

"What about you? How was your day off?" he asked.

"It was okay. I slept until noon. It was a crazy week and I'm still pretty wound up."

A sly grin crossed his face and he stood up, clearing the plates and bringing them to the sink. Then he turned to me and held out his hand.

"I've got just the thing," he said.

I eyed him warily, but stood up and took his hand. He led me through the house to the back door and I couldn't believe my eyes.

*

We stepped out onto Dave's back deck, which was huge. Set to one side was an antique clawfoot tub, complete with faucet, soap dish, and shampoo. I studied it for a moment then looked at him.

"Is that a functioning bathtub?" I asked.

"It is."

"You have a bathtub outside?"

"I do," he laughed.

"Why?"

I'd never seen anything like it, and I'd seen a lot of weird shit. Outdoor showers, yes, but an outdoor bathtub?

"I love bathing, and one night I was sitting in the tub thinking, 'this would be perfect if I could see the stars.' I've certainly got enough privacy, so why the fuck not?" he said.

I considered this. He had a point. I looked up at the stars, bright against the clear night sky. He definitely had a point.

"Want to take a bath?" he asked, startling me out of my reverie.

"It has plumbing?" I asked.

He laughed.

"Yes, it does."

"Then I think I do," I said, shocking myself.

He smiled, delighted, and reached over to turn on the tap.

"You're serious?" I said. "You're going to let me take a bath?"

"Absolutely. It's a gorgeous night, perfectly clear. You'll probably even see a shooting star or two."

When the water reached the right temperature, he put in the plug and picked up a bottle of bubble bath. I burst out laughing.

"You take bubble baths?" I choked.

He glared at me.

"Listen. There is nothing wrong with me taking baths, bubbles or no bubbles. They relax me. You want to judge me? That's on you."

I shut up. He was right. He had this quiet way of making his point that I appreciated. There was no misunderstanding the guy—he was clear and articulate. If only the guys I dated were like that.

"Sorry," I mumbled.

He nodded, indicating he heard, then shut off the water and stepped aside.

"All yours."

"You're going to leave, right?"

He rolled his eyes.

"I thought we were friends," he said.

"Friends being the optimal word here."

He heaved an exaggerated sigh and offered a smile.

"Of course. Enjoy. I'll go inside."

He turned and went back to the door, then stopped and turned back.

"Oh, wait." He walked over to the BBQ, opened the door on the hutch underneath, and took out a box. He opened it and extracted a pre-rolled joint. Smiling, he walked over and handed it to me, along with a lighter. "Enjoy."

With that, he went into the house. I stood there, watching through the window until he settled onto the couch, his back to me, and picked up his book. Satisfied, I peeled off my clothes and slipped into the tub. I closed my eyes as the water surrounded me, acting like a magnet and draining all the tension from my body.

I leaned back and opened my eyes, greeted by the night sky and the spectacular show it was putting on for me. I reached for the joint and the lighter, sparking up and inhaling deeply. If this wasn't heaven, I didn't know what was.

I'd forgotten to tie up my hair and it drifted around me in the tub, fanning out like lace. I sunk deeper, keeping my eyes on the stars. I couldn't imagine being able to do this all the time. It was no wonder Dave was such a mellow guy. Who wouldn't be with this kind of release each night? Every mocking thought I'd had earlier vanished into the night air, like the steam rolling off the water.

I had no idea how long I'd been out there, but when the chill entered my bones, I realized it was time to get out. I looked around but didn't see a towel. *Great.*

"Hey, Dave!" I called.

Luckily the windows were open.

"What's up?" he called back.

"I need a towel."

"Ha. Okay. Hold on."

He emerged a moment later and walked over to an armoire set against the side of the cottage. He opened it and pulled out a white folded towel. He brought it to me, eyes averted as the bubbles were pretty much gone by this point. I reached out and grabbed it from him and he turned away.

I stepped out of the tub, not daring to look up again until I'd wrapped the towel around me. He was back at the armoire, pulling something else out. He turned back to me and I saw it was a big, fluffy robe.

"Bubble baths, fluffy robes—you are very comfortable in your masculinity," I observed.

"I like my creature comforts," he said, shrugging.

He handed me the robe and as I reached to take it the towel slipped from around my chest. Years of working the bar had given me quick reflexes and I rectified the situation right away, but there had definitely been a moment of exposed boob. And by the blush creeping up Dave's neck, he'd caught it.

I slipped on the robe and tied the belt.

"It's only skin, dude," I said.

"Yeah," he said, breathless.

I cocked my head, studying him. He was bothered. He wouldn't meet my eye. Sure, we'd been spending a lot of time together, and I'd have been lying if I said the thought hadn't crossed my mind from time to time. But he was not my type, and he knew that. And he'd never shown any romantic interest in me. He'd just been an incredible friend. Loyal, thoughtful, kind, sweet...*Oh, shit.*

This time, when I looked at his face, he was waiting for me. We locked gazes and I saw it. For the first time, I saw it. He wanted to kiss me. I froze, unsure of what to do. *This was Dave.* And of course, the first thing to flash through my mind was Tess's story.

He took a step towards me, and I froze on the spot. Taking that as a sign of encouragement, he reached out with one hand to cup the side of my face. My breath caught. It was like I'd been touched by fire. The heat spread through my veins, coursing through my body until every part of me lit up. He drew back his hand almost immediately and I felt it. I felt the loss of his touch.

Dave?

He must have seen the confusion in my eyes and knew it was his chance. He reached out again, this time wrapping his hand around the back of my head as he brought me towards him. He bent down and brushed his lips against mine, and holy shit did my body respond. I may have whimpered as he pulled away. Our foreheads touching, he smiled at me, waiting for me to process what was going on.

"You okay?" he whispered.

I nodded slightly, not wanting to break the contact between us. He took my chin in his hand, tilting my head up as his mouth closed over mine. I shut my eyes, preparing for the worst, but it never came. Instead, what followed was the most sensual kiss I'd ever received. The man knew how to use his tongue. It took no less than three seconds for my entire body to surrender to his, and I was up on my tiptoes, pressing myself into him.

One arm came around my waist as he pulled me in closer, never breaking the kiss. My head was swimming. Despite the snail's pace with which he'd moved, I was still having trouble keeping up. *I was kissing Dave?* My arms went up around his neck, my fingers playing in his long hair. I gave a little tug and he groaned deep in his throat. *Huh, maybe crew cuts aren't the way to go.*

When we came up for air, I stared at him, unable to conceal the amazement in my eyes.

"What is it?" he asked softly, running his thumb along my lower lip.

"You're not such a terrible kisser," I whispered, trying unsuccessfully to keep the shock out of my voice.

He pulled back and stared at me.

"Thank you?" he said uncertainly. "Were you expecting me to be?"

"Yes," I said simply.

He started at that.

"Why would you assume that? Because of the way I look? The way I dress? What the fuck, Bree?"

"No," I said, feeling horrible for bringing it up. "Because of Tess."

"Because of Tess?" he asked, incredulous.

"Yes. Because—"

He put up his hand, cutting me off as the strangest look passed over his face. And then he burst into laughter so fierce he actually doubled over, holding his stomach.

"What?" I demanded. "What's so funny?"

When he finally caught his breath, he wiped a tear from the corner of his eye and looked at me, still smiling broadly.

"Tess had a thing for me. I didn't have the heart to tell her I wasn't interested. So when she finally made her move, I just gave her a really shitty kiss. I mean, really shitty. All teeth and spit. Oh my god, I can't believe she told you that."

He burst out laughing again, but this time, it was my turn to cut him off.

"Dave. Dave! What the fuck just happened?"

He grew serious and looked me dead in the eye.

"We kissed," he said simply. "And it was fucking fantastic."

I started pacing, pausing to pick up my clothes. When I strode past him, he grabbed my arm.

"Hey, are we okay?" he asked.

"I don't know. What the fuck?"

He let go of my arm and took a step back.

"Listen, I thought that was mutual. I never meant—"

"No, no," I interrupted. "That's not what I meant. It was mutual. It just shouldn't have happened. Dave. That can't happen again."

He snorted.

"Why not? That was amazing."

I let out an exasperated sigh as I bent to retrieve my shoes.

"Where can I change?" I asked.

"Bree. I asked you a question."

"And I'm standing here in your bathrobe. Where can I change?"

He turned around and made an exaggerated show of covering his eyes with his hands. I dropped the robe and towel and scrambled into my clothes.

"You can turn around," I said.

He turned to face me.

"Are you going to answer me now?"

"We're friends," I said. "That's it. I really like you, I do, and I don't want to screw this up. You are not what I'm looking for and if we go down this road I'll end up breaking your heart."

"You've got a pretty high opinion of yourself, don't you?"

"You know what I mean."

It was his turn to pace and I took a seat on the side of the tub while he gathered his thoughts. The irony wasn't lost on me, how alike we were. We'd probably have been great together. But he was too much like me, always scraping to get by. After everything I'd been through, I wanted an easy life. Someone older, dependable. Dave was someone I would've dated a decade ago.

Finally, he stopped and stood directly in front of me. He dropped to his knees and took my hands.

"Bree, I think you're making a mistake. I think we could be amazing together. You're saying that's not what you want, and I'm not going to push it, but I think you're making a mistake."

I looked down at our hands entwined in my lap. The heat spreading up my arms wasn't lost on me, but I couldn't let my hormones take over here. One of us had to keep their head. I gently extracted my hands and he sighed, rolling back on his heels before straightening up.

I stood and looked at him with a sad smile.

"Promise me we're still friends," I said.

"We're still friends. I'll even come by for a drink this week, okay?"

I nodded, still a little freaked out. I gave him a quick hug, then grabbed my bag. He walked me to my car and I drove home. Even after I crawled into bed, I knew it would be a long time before I would be able to fall asleep.

*

The first thing I did when I got to work on Tuesday evening was hand Liam a copy of my drink menu. I'd been unable to sleep the night before and the least I could do was put together the menu based on the notes I'd been taking all week.

I watched as he read it, his head nodding approvingly as he scanned down the sheet. He broke into a smile and tucked it into his apron pocket.

"Nice job, Bree. I'm going to have fun with this. You hungry?"

We were in his kitchen, Toni cleaning up after her shift and the dinner line cooks getting set up. I glanced around at the various options leftover from lunch and pointed to a pot of pasta.

"What's that?"

"It's delicious," Toni said. She walked over and spooned out a bowl for me, handing it over.

"Thank you," I said, digging in.

I was blessed to work with the two best chefs in town and it was not something I took for granted. This was my favourite time of day, coming into the kitchen during the lull, eating good food, and enjoying the company of my colleagues.

"Are there a lot of reservations tonight?" I asked.

Liam shook his head.

"Looks like a pretty quiet night, actually. Not surprising. There are fireworks in the square for something or other. I don't know what it is about fireworks that makes everyone lose their appetite."

"Don't be offended, Chef," I said. "They'll be back tomorrow."

"I'm off tomorrow," Liam said. "Toni's covering for me."

"Oh yeah? Big date?" I asked.

"Yeah. Maggie wants to double. She asked me to find someone for her friend Tammy. If it doesn't work out tomorrow, I was thinking of setting her up with Dave Winter. I saw you talking to him the other night. Decent guy, right?"

I froze when Liam mentioned Dave's name. I counted to five while my heart settled down and I answered as nonchalantly as I could.

"Yeah, great guy. But not sure Tammy's his type," I said.

I didn't miss the look Toni shot me.

"What?" I asked her.

"How do you know?" she asked.

I shrugged.

"We're friends. We've been spending some time together. He's a pretty serious guy, and Tammy just seems, well, a little flaky for him."

This time it was Toni and Liam who exchanged looks.

"Well, I don't know about that," Liam said. "I mentioned it to him the other night and he seemed pretty interested."

"When?" I asked, losing all sense of propriety.

"Why do you care?" Liam asked.

"I don't," I said, shaking it off. "You're right. It's a great idea. Have fun."

I picked up my bowl of pasta and walked out of the kitchen.

CHAPTER TWELVE

Dave

By Wednesday, I knew if I didn't text Bree, shit would start to get weird. A bunch of kids came into the store that afternoon and gathered around the merch wall. I snapped a picture of them from the back and sent it to her with the caption, *See?*

She texted back within a minute.

Yeah, but are they buying anything?

Good point.

No comment.

Uh-huh.

I laughed and tucked my phone away, then walked over to the kids to see if I could help with anything. Over the past week, I'd evolved into quite the salesman. Funny what you could do when your livelihood was on the line.

"Hey, you into the Stones?" I asked.

One of the older boys was considering a poster and his face lit up. We got into a conversation about the different stages of the Stones' career and he ended up with three albums. A couple of his buddies bought stuff, too, but this kid stayed behind when his friends left.

"Something else you need?" I asked.

"A job?" he said tentatively.

I smiled at the kid. He must have been around sixteen, jeans, concert T-shirt. He was a mini-me, except he had short hair and no tattoos.

"I wish I had something to offer you, kid. I just don't have the means to take on an employee at the moment."

He chewed on the inside of his lip for a moment.

"What if I could do it for course credit when school starts? Then you wouldn't have to pay me," he offered.

I studied him.

"What's your name?"

"Chris."

"It's nice to meet you, Chris. I'm Dave. I like your gumption."

"Gumption?"

"Never mind. Listen, I'll tell you what, you're welcome to hang out here as much as you like, and come September, make the inquiry at school. If they're cool with it, and I'm still around, great."

Chris looked at me, shocked.

"What do you mean, if you're still around?"

I shook my head. He was just a kid.

"Nothing. Just kidding. Listen, I gotta get back to work. Like I said, hang out if you like, but I can't pay you."

"Understood. Thanks, man."

*

The kid came in every day that week. First, he set to work re-organizing the merch section, bringing me half the shit he thought I should return. I almost texted Bree, knowing she'd love this kid.

We talked a bit through the day, though he tried not to disturb me when he thought I was busy. He struck me as being a world apart from his friends, who came in from time to time to tease him or try to woo him out to go hang. He always turned them down.

"What's up with that?" I asked him one morning.

"Them?" he asked, indicating his recently departed friends.

"Yeah. You never want to hang out with them."

"I hang with them plenty. But they just want to fuck around all the time. They're not serious about anything."

"Unlike you," I remarked.

He just shrugged. I liked the kid. He really did remind me of myself at his age. Not ahead of his peers, just on a different path. It had been a hard time for me, and I made a silent vow to help this kid out as much as I could.

On Saturday, at closing, I handed him a hundred bucks.

"I know it's not much," I said. "But you've really been a big help."

Chris just laughed and waved off the money.

"Dude, my folks are loaded. I don't need it. Really. I just love the music."

I stood there, holding the bill dumbly in my hands. Every time I thought I had him figured out, he threw me. I slowly tucked the money away and nodded.

"Okay then. We'll figure something else out. Why don't you grab a few albums?"

That made him smile, and like a kid in a record shop, he made his picks. I was impressed with his choices and told him so, which made him beam even more. We closed up and parted ways as he got on his bike and I headed to my car.

I'd been planning to head home, but at the last minute figured I'd pop in and have a drink with Bree. I hadn't seen her since the night she came over, and even though we'd texted almost every day, I was still worried things would be weird with us.

I pulled up in the parking lot and went inside, surprised to be greeted by Adam at the door.

"Jen off on a Saturday?" I asked.

"Nope. Bree is. Jen took the bar."

I glanced over at the bar and sure enough, Jen was back there, mixing drinks and laughing with customers. It was too late for me to walk out, so I smiled at Adam and made my way over to order a drink.

"What'll it be, Dave?" Jen asked, all smiles.

"Just a beer," I said, taking a seat. "Bree's off tonight?"

"Yup. Hot date. Some guy named—"

"Jake?"

"Yup. That's the one." Jen laughed. "She's definitely got a type, doesn't she?"

I said nothing but took a swig of my beer. She certainly did. And it wasn't me. I looked around.

"Busy night. Liam must be going full steam back there."

Jen glanced over her shoulder at the door to the kitchen.

"Actually, he's off, too. It's Toni back there. Girls' night at Cagney's, I guess," she laughed, topping up my mug.

I smiled in gratitude and took another sip as she slid the bowl of nuts towards me.

"He okay?"

"Liam? He's fine. Maggie pressured him into another double date with her friend Tammy and some new dude. He wasn't really into it, but fuck, he'd do anything for her."

I knew where he was coming from. Jen took off down the bar to serve another customer and I sat there, drinking my beer and wondering how I ended up sitting in a restaurant I'd vowed never to walk into, looking for a woman who clearly told me she wasn't interested.

I finished my drink, fished a twenty out of my wallet, and laid it on the bar. I got up, waved goodbye to Jen, and made my way back to the car.

I needed to figure some shit out.

CHAPTER THIRTEEN

Bree

Jake called sometime Saturday afternoon to so-lidify our plans. I'd been lounging on the couch, eating popcorn, and watching *When Har-ry Met Sally*. I'd had the urge to pick up the phone and call Dave, but I resisted, not wanting to give him the wrong idea. Then I got pissed that the thought had even entered my mind, and for the millionth time wondered if that kiss had ruined our friendship after all.

We'd texted a few times during the week, but it was nothing like the intense connection we'd had the week before. We dove into our friend-ship, and even though it was brief, it felt like I was missing a limb. It had been a long week at work, and each evening I'd hoped he'd come by like he promised, but he never showed. I had no one to blame but myself.

By the time Jake called, I was mentally exhausted on top of the physical exhaustion I felt from the week.

"Hey, you know what?" I said. "I was thinking maybe we'd just stay in tonight."

"Stay in?" Jake asked. "And do what?"

"I don't know. Order a pizza? Watch a movie?"

There was a moment of silence before he burst out laughing.

"Are you crazy? You deserve to be treated better than that. Get dressed up. I'm taking you somewhere nice."

We hung up and I stared at my phone. I deserved to be treated better than that? Better than what? Getting exactly what I asked for? I shook my head and thought about how when I'd told Dave how tired I was, he drew me a fucking bath and disappeared.

Why was I thinking about Dave?

I went to text him again, then stopped. What would I say if he asked what I was up to that night? I'd have to tell him, and then it would look like I'd texted him on purpose, just for the humble brag. Fuck. We had really messed this up.

I got off the couch and headed to the shower, mentally going through my wardrobe and deciding on what to wear. This was the third date with Jake, and I knew we were going to one of two restaurants, given the fact we were running out of five-star establishments to dine at. And Jake was nothing if not a five-star guy.

By the time he picked me up, I was showered, shaved, blow-dried, primped, and ready. I wore a black halter dress with a loose bodice and a pair of strappy sandals. Hair done, minimal make-up, I felt great. If somewhat tired.

As suspected, Jake drove me out to the small French bistro on the edge of town, right by the old highway.

"Have you been?" he asked.

"No," I lied. I'd been living in town for over a year and worked in the restaurant business. I'd eaten at every establishment in town, and the three neighbouring towns as well. But I knew Jake's type. He was the kind of guy who liked to be first at everything, introduce me to the finer things.

He beamed and unbuckled his seat belt. He got out of the car and I waited for him to come around to open my door. I had the routine down pat. All these guys were the same. I liked the divorced ones best. They'd invariably fucked up at some point and on their second time around, they were trying a little harder. And if they didn't have kids? Jackpot. Jake fell neatly into that category.

We walked into the restaurant and the maître d' led us to our table. He shot me a familiar smile and I made eyes at him. He instantly made his expression blank. We'd done this dance before. As we sat and picked up our menus, I saw him go over and warn our waiter, Pierre, about the situation. For the first time, I wondered what the hell I was doing. Why so much pretending? Just to please these guys?

I shook it off. Dave was getting in my head. He hadn't said as much, but I knew he disapproved of my affinity for the suits. He just didn't understand. Well, that wasn't entirely true. *Fuck.*

"I'm sorry, did you say something?" I asked, realizing I'd dropped out of the conversation.

"I was just asking if you wanted red or white?" Jake said, smiling.

"Red, please."

Jake ordered the wine, then proceeded to order dinner, despite not having asked what I wanted. I smiled politely as Pierre took our menus. I did not miss the covert look he shot me. This was too small a town. At times, I almost missed the anonymity of life before Mountain Valley and wondered why I'd tried so hard to find a place where I belonged, where people *knew* me.

"You look beautiful, Brianna."

"Bree. Thank you," I smiled tightly.

"Is Brianna not your full name? It suits you."

"It's not. Just Bree. Thanks. I love that tie," I said, a peace offering.

He touched it, adjusting it absently as he smiled at me.

"Thank you. Ties are my weakness. At least one for every occasion."

I tried to picture Dave in a tie and giggled. Jake smiled, obviously pleased that he'd made a funny joke. Pierre reappeared and poured the wine. After Jake gave his approval—despite me being the fucking bartender—Pierre poured out two glasses and retreated.

We ate mostly in silence, the meal itself pleasant enough. He asked about my work week and I asked about his. We talked about various hobbies and found we had very little in common. He had zero interest in the approaching music festival, something that shocked me. I had thought everyone in town attended. It was that huge.

He inquired about my schedule at work, hinting that he'd like to take me away for a weekend. That threw me, as he hadn't even tried to sleep with me yet. I told him I'd look into it, but the likelihood of me getting three days off in a row during the summer wasn't great.

"I'm willing to wait until fall," he said, grinning.

I froze. That was two months away. That was pretty fucking far. We'd been on three dates and he was making long-term plans?

"Let me speak to Jen and see what I can work out," I said, desperate to table the subject.

He nodded and lifted the last forkful of dessert to his mouth. He'd had an apple crumble, while I'd gone for the chocolate souffle. Who gets apple crumble at a French restaurant? At least he'd let me choose my own dessert. While the meal had been delicious, he wasn't a sharer. That pissed me off, as he ordered what I'd been eyeing on the menu. If he hadn't been interested in sampling my meal, why the hell had he felt the need to order it?

After coffee and a nightcap, we finally left the restaurant. We walked the short distance to his car, the warm July evening settling itself around us. Despite the minor aggravations, it had been a decent date. Jake took my hand, and I entwined my fingers with his. There was no immediate heat between us, but sometimes, those things took time. I was confident I could make this work.

When we got to my house, he turned off the engine and turned to me. I smiled at him, giving him my best 'come hither' look. If he didn't make a move on me, I was planning to make one on him. Granted, I'd left him rather abruptly on our first date, but the fact that he hadn't made a move on our second date left me wondering if he was a gentleman or just not into hooking up.

He reached over and brushed the hair out of my face and I leaned into his palm. He moved towards me, closing the gap between us, and kissed me softly on the mouth. I closed my eyes and tried to lose myself in the kiss, parting my lips to let him in.

I tried to go with it, but I felt...nothing. There was no heat, no fire. There were no sparks of electricity traveling through my veins. Granted, I'd never really had those things before either, but then I had. With Dave.

I pulled away, running my thumb along my lower lip, and smiled up at him sweetly.

"That was nice," I said. "Thank you."

I reached over and opened my car door.

"Bree—"

I smiled again.

"I mean it. It was really nice. Have a great night."

I opened the car door and stepped out. Without turning back, I walked up to my front door, unlocked it, and stepped inside. I closed my eyes and leaned against the door, waiting for the sound of his car pulling away. When I heard it, I exhaled the breath I'd been holding. Then I made my way upstairs.

*

"How was the date last night?" Jen asked. "Worth it?"

It was Sunday afternoon and I'd just arrived at work. As usual, I had been in the kitchen foraging for food when Jen came in.

"He was okay," I said, popping a French fry in my mouth.

Jen and Liam exchanged a look.

"You going to see him again?" Liam asked.

I shrugged.

"I don't know."

I wandered out of the kitchen and started setting up behind the bar. Toni was just coming out of the washroom, heading home after her shift. She came over and gave me a quick hug.

"Fun night?" she asked.

"Everyone keeps asking me that. It was fine," I said, perhaps a little too forcefully.

"Yeesh. Sorry. I was just curious. It's not often you take a Saturday off."

She grabbed her bag off the bar and took off. I instantly regretted my harsh words and texted her a quick apology. I wanted to talk to Toni about all this. She was my closest friend in Mountain Valley. But I'd seen what happened after Liam's love life became fodder for staff discussion last year and I didn't want to put myself through that. There were no secrets in the kitchen.

I was pulling glasses out of the dishwasher when Adam came over, waving a piece of paper.

"Hey, Bree. Got a minute?"

"Of course," I said, putting away the last two wine glasses. "What's up?"

"Liam just handed in his menu. The two of you did a fantastic job. We're going to start running it next week. We'll do a test dinner on Tuesday night after the kitchen closes. You good with that?"

I was beaming.

"Of course I'm good with that, Boss. Looking forward to it."

The dinner crowd started to trickle in as people wrapped up their lazy Sunday with a great meal. Within an hour, the bar was hopping and I had no time to dwell on the menu, Jake, Dave, or anything. It was a welcome relief, getting lost in the work. Not for the first time, I thanked my lucky stars, and hard work, that I'd managed to find something I loved to do and make money at it.

And that brought me back to Dave and his record shop. He didn't talk about it often, but I knew it was on his mind. I had no idea how he was going to save the shop, but I had my fingers crossed for him.

I had just finished serving a round of shots when I saw Maggie enter the restaurant with her friend Tammy. I stiffened slightly, remembering the conversation I'd had with Liam about Dave and Tammy. He'd also taken Saturday night off and had hinted about another double date...but I refused to take the bait. I loved Maggie, but for the first time, I had to force a smile onto my face as I walked over to greet them.

"Good evening, ladies. Can I make you a couple of drinks?" I asked.

"Yes, please," Maggie said. "You look great, Bree."

"Thanks, Mags. You, too. Heard the four of you had a night last night," I said, trying to stay casual as fuck.

A blush crept up Tammy's neck that made my skin crawl. She giggled and turned to Maggie, who burst out laughing. Tammy covered her face with her hands and Maggie shot me a look.

"She tends to fall hard," Maggie explained.

"Ah," I said.

I turned away and mixed them two drinks. I was on autopilot, to be honest, but I knew what each of them liked from previous visits, so I was pretty safe. I passed them their drinks and hightailed it to the other end of the bar. I did not need to stick around for the details as they rehashed their hot date night.

That didn't mean I didn't glance over at them from time to time, and each time I did, it annoyed me further. I should've been happy for Dave. Tammy was cute, and despite her being flaky, there was nothing wrong with her. But when I thought about Dave kissing her, or whatever he did to cause that blush to creep up her neck, it just pissed me off.

CHAPTER FOURTEEN

Dave

Monday morning, despite being Monday morning, was spectacular. The sky was clear blue, the temperature was in the low twenties, and there was zero humidity. It was the unicorn of a summer day in the Laurentians. I wanted nothing more than to be on the lake in my kayak, communing with nature and shit. Instead, I was ten minutes early to work.

Despite that, Chris was already there, waiting at the door.

"Maybe I should have a key made for you," I mumbled, working my own in the lock.

He grinned like an idiot.

"Seriously, man? That would be awesome."

"It's a perfect day, Chris. You're a sixteen-year-old kid who's working a job that doesn't pay. Why don't you take the day and go hang with your friends?"

"Nah, that's okay. Besides, there was kind of something I wanted to talk to you about."

We walked into the shop and turned on all the lights. I walked behind the counter to open the cash while Chris flipped the closed sign to open. We'd developed quite the routine in a short amount of time. It was like a well-choreographed dance. I was going to miss it.

"What's up, kid?" I asked.

"There's a girl," he said.

I laughed.

"Isn't there always? Tell me."

"I met her at Elena's the other night. I'd seen her around a few times, but it was the first time we spoke. She just moved here last year with her family. I really liked her, but I don't think she felt the same."

"I understand completely," I said, nodding.

He looked at me, surprised.

"You have trouble with girls? Dude, you're like a god."

I burst out laughing.

"To a sixteen-year-old, maybe. Not to a woman in her thirties. She sees long hair and a concert shirt and thinks, 'there's a loser with no future.'"

Chris shook his head sadly.

"I don't get women."

"Welcome to the club."

A couple of customers came in then and we broke it up so Chris could get some practice serving them. The kid was a natural and it was a joy to watch. I had horrible guilt over not paying him, but the kid was insistent, and he was happy taking home a few albums at the end of each shift. I said nothing when they were rare. He was, too, and I was no fool.

We returned to his dilemma while we ate lunch. I'd brought in sandwiches from the deli. The least I could do was feed the kid.

"The important thing is you gotta respect her," I said. "If she's not interested, there's nothing you can really do about it. If she wants to be friends, and you're cool with that, great."

"But—"

"There are no buts, kid. You pursue her against her wishes, that's stalking."

"Yeah, I get that. And she does seem to want to be friends. Does it ever…I dunno…evolve?"

I shrugged.

"Sometimes. Sometimes the longest-lasting love grows out of friendship. Sometimes, it remains unrequited. I wish there was something more I could tell you."

We both looked up as the front door opened and Bree walked in. She was a vision, wearing a light yellow sundress that contrasted dramatically against her dark hair. She turned to make sure the door shut behind her and I got a glimpse of her dual sun and moon tattoos. Then she walked up to us with a smile.

"Hey," she said. "Been a while."

"It has," I said. "It's good to see you."

She looked over at Chris.

"Who's this?"

Chris smiled and stuck out his hand with all the awkwardness a sixteen-year-old could muster. She took and it gave him a firm shake.

"I'm Chris. I'm helping Dave out in the shop."

"Well, it's nice to meet you, Chris. I'm Bree, a friend of Dave's. I didn't know he was hiring."

Chris grinned sheepishly and looked down.

"He wasn't. I kind of…insisted."

Bree burst into laughter, which was the sweetest music I'd heard all week.

"How was your weekend?" I asked casually.

A guarded look crossed her face but she forced a smile.

"Great. Just great." Then she narrowed her eyes and studied me. "How was yours?"

I shrugged.

"Same. Great."

She straightened and took in a breath as if she were about to say something, but then she just shook it off and smiled.

"What's for lunch?" she asked.

"Just sandwiches from the deli. I've got an extra. You hungry?" I asked.

She shook her head and thanked me. Another customer entered the shop, a woman in her twenties. I eyed Chris and he smiled, nodding, then walked over to greet her.

"What's that all about? I thought you couldn't afford to hire anyone?" she said quietly.

"I can't. He's not getting paid. He insisted on helping out. Loves music. Wants to see if he can get extra credit for interning here come fall."

She nodded slowly, turning to study him a little more closely.

"Nice kid?" she asked.

"The best. He's really great. And it's nice having someone around."

"I can imagine."

We both stood there silently, looking at each other. I wanted nothing more than to reach out across the counter and touch her, but I couldn't. It was killing me. The customer walked out without buying anything, but Chris stuck close to the front of the shop, busying himself with arranging some displays.

"So. What brings you here on your day off? More dry cleaning?" I smiled.

"Actually, no. The last time I was at the bookstore, I chatted with Mrs. Fairfax and I had a bit of a crazy idea. I meant to bring up sooner but kept forgetting."

"Oh yeah? What's that?"

I gathered the remnants from lunch and tossed them in the trash can. I was doing anything I could to distract myself from looking at her.

"Well, Mrs. Fairfax is in the same situation you're in, and she's got a lot of space. What if you combined shops? You could move into the bookstore and take over half the square footage. You split the rent and you'll be better off than you are now." She shrugged. "Music and books go together, don't they?"

My gut reaction was to tell her it was a ridiculous idea, but it wasn't.

"They do indeed," I said.

I didn't know what else to say. All I wanted to do was ask her about the damn date, find out if it was serious. Fuck it, what I really wanted to know was if he'd kissed her. I ran my hand over my face, trying to erase the image from my mind. Instead, what I got was me kissing her, which wasn't much better in the situation.

I looked up and offered her a weak smile. She was just staring at me, chewing her bottom lip. The air was so heavy between us, so full of unsaid things, but I just didn't know where to start. I wondered, not for the first time, if we'd irreparably damaged things with that kiss. That perfect kiss.

"Anyway, I just thought I'd mention it," she said, breaking the tension. "I should run. I've got a lot of shit to get done today."

I smiled and nodded, still unable to form any coherent words. She gave me a wave then went to the door. She touched Chris briefly on the shoulder and walked out. Chris turned to look at me.

"Who was that?"

"The friend I want more from."

Chris just stood there, blinking.

"And you think she doesn't want more from you?"

I nodded, staring out the window after her.

"I don't know, man. I'm only sixteen, but I could feel the tension from here. I'd go after her if I were you."

I looked at him, then back out the window. Without giving it another thought, I stepped out from behind the counter, speeding up as I moved through the store until I burst through the front door.

She was across the road, just about to get into her car.

"Bree, wait!" I called.

She turned to look at me, brushing her hair from her face. She tilted her head, questioning. I walked up to her, putting my hand on her wrist to prevent her from opening the car door. The sparks danced on my skin, making the hairs stand up on end. I took a deep breath.

"Listen, that was a great idea. Thank you."

She smiled brightly.

"My pleasure. Really."

She stared up at me, licking her bottom lip. I couldn't read the expression in her eyes and it was killing me. She made no move to go, but she didn't say anything else, either.

"Do you think I should go in and talk to Mrs. Fairfax? Did you bring up the idea with her?" I asked.

"Of course not. I wouldn't say a thing without mentioning it to you first. That's not my place."

"Right, of course. No. Sorry." I was already fucking this up. But she still wasn't moving. "What do you say we, uh, watch a flick or something tonight?"

I held my breath, watching the various emotions pass through her eyes. Finally, she nodded once.

"Sure. That sounds great. I'll come by around seven?"

"Perfect. I'll see you then."

With that, she got into her car and drove away. That hadn't exactly been coming clean with her, but at least it was something. I'd figure the rest out that night.

CHAPTER FIFTEEN

Bree

I drove away from Dave, turned the corner, and pulled the car over. I inhaled to a count of four, held it, then exhaled to a count of six. Yoga had never really been my thing, but I'd always found the breathing helped. Especially in moments like this, when it felt like my life was completely turned upside down.

Professionally, everything was fantastic. Personally, I was a basket case. I hadn't mentioned the date with Jake to Dave, and he certainly hadn't brought up his date with Tammy. I'd decided to proceed under the assumption that these topics were off-limits, which was weird because we were supposed to be friends. But he clearly didn't want to mention it, and I wasn't so eager, so...

I tried to put the whole thing out of my head for the rest of the day. By the time six o'clock rolled around, I was ready to hop into another shower and change for the evening. I pulled on a pair of jeans and a tank top, tying my hair up in a ponytail. No matter how hard it might be, I was going to use the evening to make things right between us. Bring us back to that friendship we'd started.

I showed up at Dave's house at seven with a large all-dressed pizza and an assortment of salty snacks. He greeted me with a hug and smile, which led me to believe he'd come to the same conclusions I had about returning to normal. I followed him into the house and put the pizza on the kitchen table while he retrieved some plates.

"Your turn to pick tonight," he said, carrying the plates into the living room.

So. There'd be no talking at all. That worked.

I followed him, placing the pizza on the table and plopping down on the couch. I turned on the TV and started scrolling, suddenly struck by how many romcoms were on offer. The last thing I wanted to watch was anything romantic or sad. I needed to find some neutral territory. Smiling, I landed on *Stand by Me*.

"Good choice," he murmured.

Unlike last time, we didn't sit together. He got comfortable in the armchair while I had the couch to myself. Distance was good. I'd already caught myself glancing in his direction a few times since I'd arrived.

We watched the movie in silence, except for the odd times when one of us would say the lines along with the character. I realized pretty early in that the movie was as meaningful to him as it had been to me. Growing up alone, I'd always been fascinated by the friendship forged by those boys.

When it was over, we both sat there for a while. He picked up his beer and drank, then looked at me with a thoughtful expression on his face.

"Thanks for that. I always loved that movie."

"Me, too."

"You never do have friends like the ones you had at twelve, do you?"

I shrugged.

"I wouldn't know."

His face fell.

"Shit, I'm sorry."

"It's okay." I laughed it off. "What does the movie mean to you?"

He paused for a moment, then got up and came to sit on the couch. Not right next to me, but not too far away.

"When I was that age, I had a group of friends. Not exactly like that, but you know, four kids I hung around with all the time. We were out one day walking in the woods one day with our slingshots, and one of the guys skimmed a bird. Broke her wing. Everyone freaked out and wanted to run. I just sat down and cried. It was the saddest thing I'd ever seen. I took off my jacket, picked up the bird, wrapped her up, and brought her home. My parents thought I was nuts, but I did all the research and called the local bird sanctuary. They guided me step-by-step and I nursed that bird back to health.

"After about a year, I was out in the backyard with her and she just flew away. No goodbye, no nothing. I should've taken it as the highest compliment, but at twelve, I was just upset that I'd lost my bird. For some reason, this movie always brings that memory back."

I studied him, seeing this rugged, long-haired, man-child in a new light. He was a provider. Just in a different way.

"That's a beautiful story," I said.

"Let me ask you something," he said.

"Anything."

"What do the tattoos mean?"

I smiled and twisted to show him the moon on my back, then turned back and pointed at the sun.

"The darkness is behind me. Only bright days ahead."

A smile blossomed across his face and it warmed my heart.

"When did you get them?" he asked.

"The day I turned eighteen. And I took it to heart."

"I can see that."

He reached over and lightly traced the rays of the sun with his fingertip. It was such a surprisingly intimate gesture and I froze, feeling the heat from his hand pass through my skin. I swallowed and looked him in the eye. He was too close.

His hand moved up my neck and around to cup my head. I closed my eyes, the butterflies soaring through my body. He pulled me closer and I felt his mouth on mine, so soft and gentle, questioning. I opened my eyes and looked at him, that same questioning mirrored in his gaze.

I parted my lips and he took my head in both hands, kissing me with an intensity that took my breath away. All reason flew from my head as I returned the kiss. I climbed into his lap, wrapping my arms around his neck as I lost myself in him, in the feeling of his hands exploring my body, his mouth over mine.

My head was swimming. I had kissed men before. It had never been like this. It was like Dave was reaching some part inside me, some part that had previously been untouchable. The spark lit deep in my belly and fire licked at my veins. I *wanted* him. I wound my fingers through his hair and he pulled gently on my ponytail and bit my neck. Passion surged through me. I closed my eyes and the image of Tammy giggling at the bar passed before me.

I sat up abruptly, breaking away. I took his arms from around me and put them down by his side. I tried to suppress the panic in my eyes, but it was hard.

"What's the matter?" he whispered.

"We can't do this."

He sighed.

"We're gonna do this again?"

"Dave. It's not just us. There are other people involved."

At that, he stiffened, too. Apparently, he didn't realize I knew about Tammy. His face shut down, his expression unreadable. I rose slowly from his lap.

"I'm not blaming you or judging you—" I started.

"I should hope not," he said, indignant.

What the hell was that about? He was the one who was technically cheating here. I had no plans to see Jake again, and for all Dave knew, I hadn't seen him since that first date.

"I just meant—"

"I know what you meant," he interrupted. "I got it. Loud and clear. Other people."

"Look, Dave, we didn't plan this."

He got up from the couch and started carrying the dishes back to the kitchen. I followed him helplessly.

"I'm at a loss here. I really don't know what to say." I felt like I was pleading with him and I hated it.

He turned to me, a deep sadness in his eyes.

"Then maybe you should just go."

CHAPTER SIXTEEN

Dave

I couldn't sleep for two nights after seeing Bree. So many times I reached for the phone to call her, but to what end? She'd made her choice clear.

On Wednesday afternoon, I was in the shop alone for a change. Chris's family was off on vacation and it felt weird working alone again. Having him around had reminded me of the old days with Jed, and I had gotten into that groove again of having someone to talk bands with during the day. And someone to watch the shop while I ran errands.

Chris's mom had come in to see me before they left, thanking me for taking care of her son. I laughed and told her he had been a huge help, that she had a great kid. She had a look of relief in her eye that made me think more than met the eye was going on. I resolved to talk to Chris when he got back.

I was unpacking a new shipment when Katie walked in sometime during the mid-afternoon.

"Well, well, look who's back," I said, greeting her with a smile.

"I'm sorry. I was in town, then out of town, now I'm back. You were my first stop."

She came over and gave me a hug and kiss, then stepped back and gave me a good once-over.

"What's wrong?" she asked.

"Nothing's wrong. Well, no, that's not true. I'm still trying to sort out the whole rent increase issue."

She put down her bag and offered me a sympathetic smile.

"I know, it's rough. I'm sorry you're going through this. Are you going to be able to hang onto the shop? I wish I had space in my building for you."

For the first time since Bree's last visit, I remembered her idea about the bookshop. My eyes must have lit up because Katie shook her head and sighed.

"Okay. There's definitely something going on."

"Yes. There is. Bree mentioned an interesting idea the other day. She thought I should speak to Isabelle Fairfax about moving into the bookshop."

Katie stopped and stared at me.

"That's a brilliant idea. Put a closed sign on the door. Let's go talk to her."

"Wait, wait. Hold up a minute. I haven't even thought this through yet."

Katie shrugged and came around the counter to hop up on the stool.

"Well, if you decide to do it, and you should, I'm happy to go with you to talk to her. I've known her my whole life. And I know you feel like a Mountain Valley boy, but she's old school. Ten years here is nothing to her. You arrived yesterday."

"Gee, thanks for the pep talk."

"It's a great idea, though. Apparently, Bree is full of them these days."

"What's that supposed to mean?" I asked.

"She didn't mention anything? Liam put together next week's tasting menu based on a selection of her cocktails. Really her moment to shine."

I stood there, blinking. She hadn't said a word to me about it.

"I had no idea," I said. "We haven't spoken that much lately."

"I thought the two of you were all buddy-buddy."

"Yeah, we were. I mean, we are. We've just both been busy. She's dating some guy. Takes up a lot of her time."

Shut up, Dave. Katie was giving me the eye, but she obviously thought better of it and said nothing.

"Well, in any case, that's one of the reasons I came in. We're booking a table. Me, Mason, Jax, Tess, Chance, Maggie, and her friend Tammy. We're an odd number. Come join us."

"Gee, what a welcoming invite."

Katie punched me on the shoulder and grinned.

"Oh, come on. Just come."

I thought about it for a moment. It would be good to be among friends, and the food would be great. Of that, I had no doubt. And it would be a good way to see Bree in a somewhat neutral setting. Maybe I'd be able to gauge where we stood if I could just see her without any expectations or pressure.

"Sure. I'll come. When?"

"Great!" she said. "Next Tuesday night. We want to be there the first night. Really show our support. Plus, we know a guy who can get us a table."

I laughed. She was referring to Adam, of course, owner of Cagney's and Tess's boy-friend. There was no way he'd launch a new menu without her there. Katie hopped off the stool and gave me a quick hug.

"Come in to see us before then. We miss you."

I smiled and promised her I would. After she left, I pulled out a piece of paper and jotted down some talking notes for Isabelle Fairfax. It was a good idea. That bookstore was huge and I had way too much inventory that wasn't sell-ing. At four o'clock, I hung the Closed sign on the door with a hand-scrawled apology and made my way down to Main Street.

*

I walked into the bookstore and Mrs. Fairfax was standing behind the cash, ringing up a sale. When the customer left, I approached her and she greeted me with a wide smile.

"Why Mr. Winter. How are you?"

"I'm just great, Mrs. F. How are you?"

"Just fine. You adjusting to Mountain Valley yet?"

I laughed. Katie hadn't been joking.

"It's been ten years now, but yes, I'm adjusting nicely. Thank you for asking."

"What brings you in today? Looking for a particular book?" she asked.

"Actually, no. I came in to talk to you about something a little bigger. You have a moment?" I asked.

She looked around and saw a few customers browsing the shelves. She turned to me and smiled.

"Sure. What is it?"

"Well, without being insensitive, I understand we're both in similar positions with this upcoming rent hike."

She nodded her head sadly but said nothing, waiting for me to go on.

"Well, I don't know about you, but I certainly won't be able to afford the rent on my shop. I hate the idea of going out of business, but there aren't many other options here. At least not ones that are vacant at the moment."

"I hear what you're saying. Just the thought of having to pack all this up...forget it. My grandson keeps telling me to sell the business, but then what would I do? I'm not ready to retire. I love this store."

She sighed and straightened a few books on the counter display.

"What if I moved in?" I said bluntly.

She stopped what she was doing and looked at me.

"With your records?" she asked. I nodded. "Well, that's an interesting idea."

She said nothing for a few moments as she turned it over in her head. I could practically see the wheels turning.

"How would that work?" she asked.

"Well, I don't need that much space, to be honest. There's a lot of inventory I could do without." I turned to face the back of the store. "I could take the space at the back, over there, and we could make a clear delineation between the shops. Or not. There's something to be said for mixing the two art forms. We'd split the rent according to the square footage being used."

She paused for a moment.

"Your hair is very long," she said finally.

"It comes with the career choice," I said. "Consider it part of the uniform."

She said nothing but rubbed her chin with her fist.

"Let me think about it. I'll discuss it with my grandson and see what he has to say. It would be nice to have someone around again, now that I had to let Shane go."

An ace up my sleeve.

"I've got a kid working with me at the moment. I can't afford to pay him, but with the rent reduction, maybe the two of us could swing some hours for him. He's a great kid. Responsible, clean-cut," I added, smiling.

She nodded, starting to warm to the idea.

"It would be nice to have someone else unpack the boxes for me. I'm not a spring chicken anymore."

"You look just fine to me, Mrs. F."

"You have a family?" she asked, then hurriedly continued. "No, I guess not. Small town like this, I'd know about it. You people take so long to settle down these days."

I smiled patiently, seeing my future unfold before me if I moved into this shop. But it was worth it to save the business.

"All right, young man. Let me talk to my grandson and I'll get back to you."

She put out her hand and I took it, shaking it first, then turning it to kiss the back. I looked up at her and she blushed, taking her hand back shyly.

"I'll have to watch out for you," she said, shaking her head with a gleam in her eye.

CHAPTER SEVENTEEN

Bree

The noise at the bar had grown so loud it was almost impossible to distinguish one voice from the next. It was a big crowd for a Thursday night, even in the summer. The air-conditioned restaurant was a preferable option to the heat outside, especially when I was behind the bar mixing drinks.

I welcomed the distraction. I'd been a bundle of nerves all week. First the blow-out with Dave, then the test-run on the tasting menu — which went great — and then the anticipation of the launch. I was happy to be in the zone, doing my thing, and making people happy.

Then I looked up and saw Jake. I flashed him a smile and busied myself with some dirty glasses before going over to see him. I hadn't spoken to him since that last date. I'd avoided his calls and texts altogether. I knew it was poor behaviour on my part, but it was just one more thing for me to deal with.

I wiped my hands on my apron and walked over.

"Can I fix you a drink?" I asked.

"You can give me an explanation," he countered.

I glanced around, but of course, no one seemed to need me at that moment.

"I'm sorry, Jake. I am. You're a great guy. I shouldn't have ghosted you like that."

"Was there a reason? Was it something I did?" he asked.

"No, not at all. To be honest, I'm going through a lot of shit right now, and—"

"Bree, why didn't you say anything? Maybe I can help."

I melted at his words. Those were exactly the words I longed to hear from a man. Some version of "Relax, let me take care of it for you." I looked at him, appraising him once again and asking myself why I didn't give him a fair shake. Then I remembered the kiss. Shamefully, I was torn. Was chemistry that important? Was sex that important?

"No, I don't think so," I said kindly. "But thank you for asking. Now let me get you that drink."

I turned away to mix him a cocktail before things could progress any further. I served him, then moved down the bar.

While tending to other customers, I watched him nurse his drink and chat with Adam. I was curious to know what they were talking about, but not enough to make my way over and give him any false hope. I had to maintain distance. It was the best way. He'd figure it out.

"Lots going in that brain of yours?"

I jumped at the sound of Jen's voice in my ear and turned to see her grinning behind me. She was pulling on an apron.

"What's up?" I asked. I checked the clock. It was only ten. "You bored?"

"You're off," she said. "No more reservations, so I can take over. Why don't you go home and get some sleep?"

I threw my arms around her neck and hugged her, hearing her laughter echo in my ear.

"Go," she whispered. "I'll make sure Jake doesn't follow you out."

I gave her an extra squeeze then walked casually into the kitchen. As soon as I was safely inside, I ripped off my apron and tossed it towards the hamper in the corner.

"Off early?" Liam asked.

"Yup. Jen stepped in for me. You should be done any minute now."

A look of relief passed over his face.

"Maggie's been waiting for me at home. Some news she wanted to share but refused to tell me over the phone. I'll be glad to get out of here."

Just then, Adam walked through the kitchen doors and nodded at Liam.

"You've got three more tables coming, then you're done for the night."

Liam let out a whoop and took the orders from the server who'd followed Adam into the kitchen. Liam was old-school, refusing to use a computer-based ordering system. He insisted on human interaction as much as possible. If nothing else, it made for a really tight staff.

Adam turned to me as I grabbed my bag.

"Oh, Bree, we're sold out for Tuesday night."

I turned to him, stunned.

"Get out. I thought we had at least a few tables left."

"Nope. I was holding one for the Franni's gang, and then I just gave the last one to that group of bankers. But I found a spot for Jake, too. You know him, right?" Adam grinned.

"You did not. Fuck. I've been trying to ditch him."

The smile dropped from Adam's face.

"I'm sorry. I thought things were going well. He's a great customer. Shit. I'm really sorry."

I sighed.

"It's fine. I'll be busy behind the bar, he'll be seated at a table. It's all good."

Adam swallowed.

"What?" I asked.

"He asked to be seated at the bar."

*

The bar was packed all weekend. People were trickling into town early for the Mountain Valley Music Festival that took place in mid-August. It was brilliant timing for the launch of the tasting menu, as we had a whole new crowd to feed.

Maggie was still keeping a few shifts at The Elway, even though her writing career was going well. She felt it kept her grounded and some of the shit she found in the rooms made great fodder for subplots. She'd been keeping tabs on all the musicians who were due to check in over the coming weeks and it was shaping up to be a pretty great end-of-summer party.

Sunday night was no exception from the rest of the weekend and more than once Jen had to give me hand behind the bar.

"You're a little off," she commented at one point, as I reached for the wrong bottle.

"I know," I admitted.

"Want to talk about it?" she asked.

I glanced at the busy bar.

"Not right now."

She nodded, understanding, and we both got back to work. At one point in the evening, Tess came in to wait for Adam and she was soon joined by Katie and Jax. I went over and brought them a round of cocktails.

"You all having fun?" I asked.

"Yes. We just had a great dinner. Thanks for these," Katie said, indicating the drinks.

I poured myself a shot and toasted them, and we all drank together. The three of them had something special going on, much like we did at the restaurant, but they had years of history between them. Watching the three of them was like watching aliens speak in a different language. They just got each other. I'd noticed over the past year that Chance had slowly been joining in with them, but he'd been taking his time coming out of his shell. Not for the first time I made a mental note to keep an eye on the female customers.

"Where's Chance tonight?" I asked.

"He's home. He's opening," Jax said.

"Awfully late for you all to be out when at least one of you is joining him," I said.

With that, Jax slid off the barstool and passed the rest of his drink to Tess.

"Party pooper," he said, throwing me a kiss.

"Hey, you don't have to leave," I called after him. I turned to the two women. "Shit. Sorry."

They both laughed.

"Don't worry about it. We told him to leave an hour ago when we finished eating," Tess said.

I stood chatting with the two of them for a few minutes while I cleared the empty glasses and wiped down the bar. Then I left them to their drinks as I served another customer. I glanced up at the clock. Another hour and I'd be out of there. I was looking forward to the day off, especially given the pressure of Tuesday's launch and the knowledge of the packed house.

Jen came over and put her arm around my shoulder.

"You know what? I got it from here. Why don't you head home?"

"You sure?" I asked.

"Positive. But I'm calling you tomorrow. We're having lunch. I want to know what's going on with you."

I smiled gratefully and hugged her. Then I peeled off my apron and walked out from behind the bar.

CHAPTER EIGHTEEN

Dave

Monday morning Chris was in the shop when I arrived and the smile that broke out across my face was almost embarrassing. I'd missed the kid, and it was good to have him back.

"Hey, how was your vacation?" I asked.

He smiled sheepishly.

"So, here's the thing. Wasn't really a vacation," he started.

We entered the shop, flipping on the lights as we moved through towards the back. I put down my bag and pulled up the stool. I sat, waiting for him to continue.

"I got myself into a little trouble at school last year. Vandalizing, if you want to be precise." He looked down at his hands, ashamed. "I got in with the wrong crowd for a while and things went south. My parents and I made a deal—I found myself something constructive to do and agreed to go to a "camp" for a week during the summer, and we could start with a clean slate."

I stared at him, stunned. This was the nicest, most responsible kid I'd ever met, and he was telling me he was some kind of vandal?

"What the fuck happened, Chris?" I asked.

"It was a tough time for me. I don't know. It wasn't like me at all, and I understand a lot more about my motivations after the past week. But please don't fire me, Dave. I swear I'm not like that."

I softened immediately.

"Kid, I'm not firing you. I'm glad you told me all this, but that's not the Chris I know. I judge by what I see, and so far, you've been an exemplary employee. Or should I say, volunteer?"

Chris laughed, breaking the tension.

"Honestly, I'm just glad you worked your way through it, and I could be here to help. The guy who used to own this shop set me on the straight and narrow, and I'm kinda glad to return the favour."

"What a relief. Thanks, man."

I smiled, hopped off the stool, and went to grab a folded box from the corner.

"Now that that's taken care of, why don't you get started packing? Make sure you label the contents of each box."

I handed him a box and a marker while he just looked at me, confused.

"What's going on? You shutting down?"

I smiled.

"Nope. We're moving. I struck a deal with Mrs. Fairfax and her grandson, owners of the bookshop across the square from Main Street. We're taking over the back space and splitting the rent. With the money we're both saving, we can afford to pay you part-time hours during the school year."

Chris's face lit up and he grabbed the box and marker.

"Boss, that's the best news I've heard all day. I'll get started right away."

*

The day progressed at a slow and steady pace. We didn't have a lot of customers, but that was actually a godsend. We had four days to pack up before the movers came on Thursday. My goal was to not lose any time afterward, as it was peak music festival season.

Sometime during the afternoon, Katie came in holding a box from the bakery. She stopped short, surveying the scene before her.

"What's going on?" she asked cautiously.

I looked up, a mischievous grin on my face.

"What? The all-knowing Katie is in the dark?" I asked.

Chris looked up from taping a box and waved at her. She returned the wave then turned back to me.

"Seriously. You're not closing. I'd have heard if you were closing."

"Nope," I said, straightening up. "I took your advice and spoke to Fairfax. I'm moving in with her."

Katie's eyes lit up and she jumped up and down, clapping her hands.

"Oh, Dave, I'm so happy for you. But it wasn't really my idea. I thought Bree had come up with it."

I shrugged.

"Technicality."

"No, it's not. And you can thank her tomorrow when we go to dinner."

Right. Dinner. Not like I'd forgotten. Seeing her again had been on my mind for the past week, since Katie had brought it up the first time. I hadn't screwed up enough courage to go into the restaurant since, but there'd be no excuses now.

"You sure you've still got room at the table for me?" I asked.

She glared at me, eyes narrowing.

"You are not getting out of this. What the hell is going on, Dave?"

I glanced over at Chris, who just shrugged at me. I turned back to Katie.

"Have time for a quick walk?" I asked.

She nodded and took me by the elbow, leading me out of the store. Before we left, she turned to Chris.

"There are donuts in the box on the counter. Help yourself."

Chris leapt up and smiled, thanking her profusely as he made a beeline to the box.

The two of us walked outside, the humidity hitting me like a wall of heat.

"Whoa," I said.

"Yeah. I cannot understand how you wear jeans all summer."

I glanced over at Katie, clad in only a light summer dress and sandals. I reached over and tousled her hair and she swatted me on the chest.

"Most guys with abs like that would show them off, you know. Not hide them behind loose-fitting concert T-shirts."

"I guess I'm not most guys," I said.

"That you're not. Want to tell me what's bugging you?"

We sat down on a bench across from the ice cream parlour and Katie gave me her complete attention.

"I fell in love with a girl," I said simply.

"Quoting Jack White, are we?"

"I'm serious."

She turned to me, eyes wide.

"Dave. We've known each other for years. I've never known you to do anything but casually date. Who's the girl?"

I didn't answer her right away.

"The casual dating wasn't by choice. I just never met anyone I cared enough about to get serious with. And now that I have, she's not interested."

"Are you sure?"

"Positive. Not only is she not interested, she's seeing someone else."

"Oh. That definitely throws a wrench into things. You going to tell me who it is?"

I thought for a moment.

"Not yet."

"Someone I know?" she probed.

I just shrugged. She sighed and took a minute to watch a small child negotiate a huge waffle cone. We both smiled as we watched the poor kid. His desire was far outweighed by his poor motor skills.

"Well, you'll tell me when you're ready. In the meanwhile, you'll come out with us tomorrow night and have a great time. I promise. Have you met Tammy?"

I shook my head.

"I don't think so. She's the one who works with Maggie at The Elway, right?" I asked.

"That's the one. She's sweet, and I'd say she could've been a nice diversion, but I hear she's off the market. Maggie and Liam took her out on a double date a while back with some guy who works with Mason. She is smitten."

"Is he joining us?" I asked, not anxious to watch two people fawning over each other all evening while I ate.

"Nope. He's actually out of town with Mason."

"I thought Mason was coming. Wasn't I rounding out the table?" I asked.

"He was, but now he's not. Life with a movie star. What can I say?"

She shrugged and stood up, smoothing out her dress before turning to me with a smile.

"I'm going to let you get back to work. If you ever decide you want to discuss this further, you know where to find me."

She leaned down and gave me a kiss on the forehead, then took off down the road.

CHAPTER NINETEEN

Bree

Game night.

I got to the restaurant early and was excited to see how gorgeous the place looked. Adam had swapped out the regular table clothes and replaced them with dark blue ones, casting a whole different tone over the room. White dishes, white flowers, and lit candles everywhere.

Dinner service was due to start in half an hour, and I took my place behind the bar to set up. I had abandoned my uniform of black jeans and a tank top for the night in favour of a tight black dress with tiny straps and a pair of black heels. It was a special occasion, after all.

Liam came up behind me and grabbed my waist, dropping a kiss on my neck.

"You look smoking hot, Bree," he said.

I turned to face him and stroked his cheek.

"Likewise," I said.

Liam had traded in his usual white uniform for a black one and he looked outrageously handsome. Maggie was in for a treat when she saw him. Just as I was about to voice that thought, she walked into the restaurant, looking resplendent in a green dress set against her red hair. I raised my eyebrows and nodded my chin towards her.

Liam turned his head and his entire body sagged. He reached out for the bar as a dopey smile spread across his face. I laughed.

"You're fucking pathetic, Chef, you know that?" I said.

Directly behind her followed Katie, Tess, Jax, Chance, Tammy, and...holy shit. Dave. I swallowed and possibly turned pale because Liam reached out and took my elbow.

"You okay?" he asked.

I nodded.

"Yeah. Sure. I'm fine. That's quite the table," I said, indicating the group walking towards the middle of the restaurant.

Liam smiled.

"Yeah, they wanted to come in as a group on the first night to support us. Nice to have such good friends, isn't it?"

I forced a tight smile as I watched Dave take a seat next to Tammy. I stiffened slightly, and Liam eyed me.

"You okay?" he asked.

"Yeah, fine."

He glanced over at the table, his gaze lingering over Dave, then back at me.

"Anything going on I should know about?" he asked.

"Don't be ridiculous," I said. "Besides, shouldn't you be in the kitchen?"

He gave me a quick salute, then a kiss on the cheek before taking off through the swinging doors.

As the restaurant filled, I started mixing drinks and setting them out on the bar. Liam and I were in perfect sync, and every time a server would come out of the kitchen with tapas on her tray, she'd stop to pick up the accompanying cocktails. Before long, the noise level in the restaurant was through the roof as people ate and drank with reckless abandon. It was a beautiful sight to behold.

As I was setting out the next round, I looked up and saw Jake slide into his stool across from me. I took a deep breath and smiled at him.

"Hey, Bree," he said.

"Good evening, Jake. So glad you could be here."

He leaned forward across the bar and brushed my cheek.

"Are you?"

I took his hand and lowered it.

"I am. But listen. I'm sorry if I haven't been clear. I'm not interested in pursuing anything with you right now. We had a lovely time, let's leave it at that."

He offered me a pained smile and I passed him a drink. Just as I did, Stella, one of the servers, appeared and slid a plate of tapas under his nose. We really were in sync. I turned away from Jake and found myself looking right at Dave's table. They were all talking and laughing, clearly having a great time. There was no bodily contact between Tammy and Dave, but he did turn to her whenever she spoke.

I was about to turn away when he looked over and caught my eye. The entire restaurant vanished as we stood there, gazing at each other, unable to say a word. I could feel the air charging between us, building until I could feel it pulsing through my veins. I took a deep breath and held onto the bar, not breaking eye contact.

Then Tammy laughed at something and Dave looked at her, breaking the spell. The din from the crowd returned and I looked over to see Stella waiting on me, clearly confused that I was behind in my duties. I snapped out of it and got the drinks on the tray for her. She clicked her heels as she walked off and I laughed to myself, making a note to make her a killer drink at the end of her shift.

The night went by quickly, but every time I passed Jake, he made some comment or another, obliging me to stop and chat with him. I was cursing Adam in my head and resolved to never let any of the staff know anything about me ever again. Ever. Jen came behind the bar and tied on an apron.

"You haven't peed all night," she said. "Go take a break. I've got you covered for the next twenty minutes."

I looked at her in relief.

"You sure? You know the drinks, right?"

"I've got it. Go."

I pulled off my apron and made my way to the kitchen first. Liam high-fived me as I walked through the door and started shoving food in my face. I laughed around a mouthful of tapas then brushed away the crumbs as I headed back out to the restrooms.

Once done, I took a look in the mirror, fixing my hair and my lipstick before going back out to the crowds. I smiled. The night had been a raging success. Everyone was having a great time. I had made my mark on this fucking town.

Smiling, I walked out of the bathroom and straight into Dave.

He caught me by the elbows and looked down at me.

"Bree."

"Dave."

My voice was little more than a whisper. I couldn't hear anything over the sound of my heart beating, which was suddenly going a hundred miles an hour. My throat was dry and for some reason, I couldn't stop blinking. I reached out and put my hands on his chest, just to make sure he was real. He groaned.

"Bree."

"You said that already."

We looked at each other, his hands on my arms, mine resting on his chest. There was so little space between us, no room at all to breathe. I could see a thin sheen of sweat break out on his forehead and God help me, I wanted to lick it off. My hand, seemingly with a mind of its own, started to move across his chest, tracing the lines of his well-defined muscles. I sighed and he let go of my elbows to grab my wrists.

"What are you doing?" he asked.

"I don't know. I can't help myself," I said, looking at him with pleading eyes.

He pulled me in and crushed his lips against mine. There was no tenderness, no tentative brush—this was a whole different kind of kiss. This kiss was a demand. My arms went up around his neck as his went around my waist. Without breaking the kiss, I walked him back inside the women's restroom. He pushed me up against the door and I pressed my body into his, grinding my hips against him as he growled deep in his throat.

"Fuck, Bree."

I reached over and locked the door. He grabbed me around the waist and I jumped up, wrapping my legs around him. He walked me over to the sink and put me down on the counter where he kissed me again, his hands everywhere. I pulled away, placing my palms on his chest and pushing him back.

"Tammy," I said.

He looked at me, completely confused.

"Who?"

"Tammy."

He turned around to see if anyone else was in the bathroom with us.

"Who the fuck is Tammy?" he asked.

"The woman sitting next to you at your table."

Confusion still clouded his eyes.

"Your date," I clarified.

He stepped back, stunned.

"My date? I never met the woman before to-night. She's a friend of Maggie's." He studied me. "Bree, what are you talking about?"

It was my turn to be confused.

"Didn't you double-date with her and Maggie and Liam a few weeks back?" I asked.

He shook his head.

"No, that was some friend of Mason's. She hasn't shut up about him all night."

I still didn't get it.

"But wait. When we were together last time, and I said there were other people to consider—"

"Jake," he said simply.

It was a complete role reversal. I felt like he must've felt seconds ago.

"Jake?" I said. "I'm not dating Jake."

"So, what's he doing here? All night you've been—"

I put my finger against his mouth.

"Misunderstandings. All of it. The whole time."

He looked at me, realization dawning in his eyes. He looked me up and down once, then reached forward and pushed the strap of my dress down my shoulder as he dipped his head and kissed my tattoo. My hands went around his head as he carefully used his tongue to trace each ray of sunshine. I melted into a puddle. When he was done, he looked up at me.

"I've been wanting to do that from the first moment I saw you," he whispered.

He raised his head and took my face in his hands. I stared into his eyes as he gazed at me with hunger, desire, and a careful measure of tenderness. I traced the curve of his mouth with my fingertip and he grabbed my hand, leaning in and covering my mouth with his.

There was a noise outside in the hallway but we both ignored it as he tore at the other strap of my dress. Before long, he'd pushed the front down entirely, exposing my breasts. He reached out, skimming his fingers across my nipple. I shivered and he smiled at me before cupping me completely. I reached for him, pulling his shirt up over his head as I once again marvelled at the beauty of his chest. It was a goddamn work of art. And I wasn't talking about the tattoos.

I ran my hands over his stomach and I felt his abs tighten, his pulse beating hard and strong through the warmth of his flesh. He bent down and took my nipple in his mouth, causing me to cry out in a way that had him reach up with his hand to cover my mouth. He pushed me back against the mirror and I braced my heels against his ass. This was not sex with suits. This was on a completely different level.

He broke away from my mouth to drop a row of kisses along the side of my neck up to my ear.

"The things you do to me," he growled in my ear.

The warmth spread between my thighs. I was so incredibly turned on. He put his hands on my legs, pushing my dress up until it was bunched up around my waist.

"Fuck, Bree. Where are your panties?"

I shrugged.

"I don't like lines."

He closed his eyes for a moment, taking a deep breath before opening them again and looking deep into my eyes, that hunger having replaced everything else. I'd never felt so wanted in my life and it was an incredible aphrodisiac.

His hand resting on my inner thigh, he ran his thumb up between my legs, causing my hips to rise off the counter. It was like a bolt of electricity shot through me. A flush of heat raced through me and I moaned, leaning my head back against the mirror. He grinned, dipping his head between my thighs, running his tongue along my most sensitive parts.

"Oh, god, Dave."

He spread my legs apart with his hands, bending down to get as comfortable as possible, given the circumstances. His mouth closed over me and stars exploded in my head. This was definitely not sex with suits. For years, my life had consisted of dark bedrooms, missionary position, and a peck on the forehead afterward. This was not that.

I clutched his hair as his tongue found my clit, coaxing it into his mouth as I pulled his head in closer. He sucked lightly and I made a sound I'd never heard come out of me before. He glanced up and grinned before getting back to work. Without warning, the orgasm plowed through me at full steam. I cried out and he once again threw a hand over my mouth, which I proceeded to bite down on. My legs were locked around his neck, his mouth bringing me to incredible heights.

He drew back slowly as I came down, kissing his way down my leg to my knee as he pulled at his belt.

"Dave," I breathed.

He looked at me, that hunger still there, increased tenfold if possible. He dropped his pants to his ankles and stepped back up to me, grabbing me around the waist and pulling me across the counter towards him. My dress was gathered around my waist, both my upper and lower half completely exposed. He was, for all intents and purposes, naked. There was a knock on the door.

"Five minutes," I called.

Footsteps retreated and I looked back at him, laughing. He wasn't laughing. And the lust in his eyes wiped the smile from my face. I took his head in my hands and kissed him, deepening the kiss as I tasted myself on him, getting more and more turned on by the second.

I reached down and took him in hand. He was rock hard, the head of his cock already glistening. My breath was coming fast and short as I anticipated what was coming. I'd never wanted anyone, or anything, more than I wanted Dave at that moment. I looked up to find him gazing at me, eyes now filled with wonder.

"Condom?" I asked.

His face dropped. I closed my eyes.

"Please tell me you have a condom," I said again.

"I don't," he whispered, frustration clear in his voice. I studied him for a second, my hormones in complete control.

"You clean?" I asked.

He nodded.

"I haven't had sex in over a year. You?" he asked.

"I'm clean. And it's not the right time in my cycle to get knocked up."

We looked at each other, unable to believe what we were about to do, but way too consumed with lust to do anything but. With one sure move, Dave pulled me towards him as I reached down and guided him in. I sucked in my breath as entered, wrapping my legs around him again, enjoying the feel of him inside me.

"You feel so fucking good," he groaned.

"Fuck me," I pleaded.

Wasting no time, he held me by the hips and started moving in and out, slowly at first, then faster as both our breathing came quicker and quicker. It was bright as day in the bathroom and we were watching each other intently, something I'd never done before but which was adding a whole other layer of sensation to the experience.

He glanced down between us, to where we were joined, and I let my hand drop, running my finger against the length of his cock as he withdrew before thrusting back into me again. My finger found my clit and I touched myself as he watched, his body growing tense as he approached his release. Watching him watch me made me feel wanton as hell and I felt my second orgasm build as his rhythm intensified.

"Oh, fuck, I'm going to come again," I cried.

His mouth came down on me, his tongue finding mine as my body erupted once again. I clamped my legs around him, sucking his bottom lip as the aftershocks rolled through my body. I dug my nails into his back and his hips snapped against the counter as he came deep within me. He dropped his head to my shoulder, breathing deeply and peppering my neck with kisses.

"That was incredible," I muttered, head still spinning.

He pulled back and looked at me.

"You are somehow even more exquisite than I imagined."

I looked down and straightened my straps as he reached for his jeans. When he looked back up, he burst into laughter.

"Are you blushing? Did I make Bree Rollings blush?" he asked, delighted.

"Shut up," I said, jumping down off the counter.

I pulled down my dress as he found his shirt and put it on. Shame. Both dressed, we looked each other up and down, checking for obvious signs of hanky panky. I smiled up at him and he reached over to once again trace the lines of my tattoo.

"You really like that, don't you?" I said. He just nodded.

I reached out and combed through his hair with my fingers.

"You ever think about cutting it?" I asked quietly.

"Do you want me to?"

I shook my head. He smiled. I turned to the mirror and fixed my hair, then pulled out my lipstick and reapplied. I glanced at his reflection.

"You go out first. Give me a minute to clean up."

"Yes, ma'am."

I turned, reached up, and kissed him softly on the mouth.

"You going to wait for closing?"

"Abso-fucking-lutely."

*

I waited a few minutes and let myself out, making my way down the short passageway back to the bar. I smoothed out my dress, trying to keep it casual, but my heart was beating a million miles an hour.

As soon as I stepped back behind the bar, Jen turned to me, all sensors on.

"Where were you?"

"You told me to take a break," I said.

She looked me up and down slowly, despite the crowd of customers waiting for their drinks. Then she cocked her head to one side.

"Something's different."

I waved her off.

"I don't know what you're talking about," I said, walking past her to retrieve my apron.

She whipped around and grabbed my arm, preventing me from moving further away. Then she leaned in and hissed in my ear.

"You reek of sex."

I stood up straight, feeling that blush creep up my neck again. Her eyes widened and her jaw dropped.

"Who?" she demanded.

I said nothing. She pushed me aside and walked to the end of the bar, looking down the hall towards the bathroom door. I thanked God Dave had left first.

Jen whipped her head back around and surveyed the restaurant, eyes like a hawk. She stopped at Dave's table and at just that moment he glanced over at me. She nodded and turned to me, a huge-ass grin breaking out on her face.

"I LOVE that guy. What a great choice," she said warmly.

I rolled my eyes.

172

"I fucked him in the bathroom on the biggest night of my life. It means nothing more than that."

"Uh-huh," she said, still sporting that shit-eating grin. "I'm sure that's all it was."

CHAPTER TWENTY

Dave

I somehow managed to get through the rest of dinner without exploding and bid everyone goodnight at the door. Well, everyone except Maggie and Tess, both of whom were curious as to why I wasn't leaving.

"I'm just going to grab a drink," I said, pointing towards the bar.

The two of them looked at each other, then over at the bar. Tess let out a little knowing snort and clapped me on the back.

"Yeah, good luck with that. You're not quite her type."

I smiled, saying nothing, and took my leave. They both headed back into the kitchen while I sat down and waited for Bree to come over.

She was serving a customer at the other end of the bar, but as if she sensed me she turned around and saw me staring at her. She threw me a smile before turning back to the guy and his drink order. As I watched her, she started slowly swaying her hips. Side to side at first, then in a tight circle. It was subtle, and completely out of sight to anyone without my vantage point, but she knew exactly what she was doing.

I shifted on the stool and a moment later, her hand dropped and she smoothed her dress out over her hip. Then her hand moved to the back and performed the same action over her ass, lingering for a moment before coming back up. My cock was rock hard, especially knowing she wasn't wearing anything under that dress. I was having trouble breathing.

After what seemed like an eternity, she turned around and walked toward me, stopping midway down the bar to draw me a beer. By the time she reached me, she was flushed and her nipples were strained against her dress. She passed me the beer and our fingers brushed, causing both of us to seek out each other's eyes.

"Get those nipples in check," I murmured.

She smiled, glancing down.

"I can't fucking help it. I can't stop thinking about—"

"Trust me, I know." I looked around. The restaurant was emptying. "How much longer?"

She glanced at the clock.

"Forty-five minutes? The staff's going to want to celebrate after."

I shut my eyes. This was fucking torture. I wanted nothing more than to get my hands on her body again.

"You're going to come home with me after," I said, a statement more than a question.

She smiled and chewed her lower lip.

"Are you going to do that thing with your tongue again?"

My cock sprang to attention. I leaned forward on the bar until we were inches apart.

"And much more," I whispered.

"I'll make it quick," she promised.

*

True to her word, we were out of the restaurant an hour and a half later. She slipped away with Jen for a moment after closing, and once the staff and hangers-on were sufficiently drunk, Jen took over at the bar and Bree and I slipped out the back door.

As soon as we were outside, I pushed her up against the brick wall and kissed her. She melted into me, and it felt like every wish I'd ever made came true in that instant.

"I'll have to tell Tess how wrong she was," Bree murmured into my neck.

I kissed her again and she responded, winding her arms around me, fingers finding their way through my hair. I had my palms against the wall, her small frame pressed between me and the brick. I could feel every inch of her as her body strained towards mine. I kissed a line down her neck towards the hollow of her throat. She moaned softly, fisting my hair in her hand.

"We have to go," she sighed.

"Where do we have to go?" I murmured, nuzzling her cleavage.

"Home. One round of public sex is my limit per night."

I put my hands on her hips and pulled her away from the wall, towards me.

"Not if you're going to be having sex with me, it's not." I kissed her. "But I'll go easy on you. Your place or mine?"

"Yours," she said, without hesitation.

"You're thinking about a bath, aren't you?"

"Am I that transparent?" she asked.

I eyed her up and down.

"I wish that fucking dress was."

She laughed and took my hand, leading me to her car.

*

"The truth is," I said, sliding my arm around her waist and letting my hand fall between her legs, "the bath is the worst place to have sex. Very inconvenient. It's excellent, however, for a little manual stimulation."

Bree moaned and relaxed against me in the tub. It was a gorgeous night and we were soaking in a sea of bubbles under the stars. She was sandwiched between my legs, her back to my chest, and despite the bathwater, I could feel how slick and ready she was for me.

"Is this not how the suits did it?" I teased.

"Can you shut up about the suits, please?"

I smiled and brought my other hand around to cup her breast. She lay her head on my shoulder and closed her eyes and there was nothing better than watching her as I brought her to orgasm.

"This is sinful," she sighed, reaching back to stroke my face.

I took her hand and kissed each of her fingers.

"Want me to do it again?"

She chuckled.

"Maybe, but I was talking about the fact that we're bathing naked outdoors."

"Enjoy it," I said. "It's not quite the same experience in the dead of winter."

She twisted her head to look at me.

"Has it really been a year since you've had sex?" she asked.

"Shut up," I said. "Just be grateful I don't sleep around."

She laughed, delighted.

"But you're so good at it," she teased.

I deflected by changing the subject.

"So?" I asked. "The evening was a success?"

"I'll say!"

It was my turn to laugh.

"I meant at the restaurant. The dinner. I imagine this was a huge deal for you."

She pulled away from me and turned around, resting her back against the opposite sides of the tub. I took her foot in my hand and started massaging it. She moaned in pleasure.

"That feels...amazing. Thank you. And yes, the dinner was a huge success. I'm proud."

"You should be," I said. "The two of you did a great job. I can't remember the last time I had a better meal."

"Thanks. How's everything going with you? The shop?"

"I'm packing up," I said.

She sat up in the tub, water splashing over the rim onto the deck.

"What? What's going on?"

I smiled.

"I'm moving into the bookstore."

Her body sagged with relief.

"Oh, Dave, that's fantastic. It'll be the best thing. You'll see. When's the move?"

"Thursday."

She blinked.

"Holy shit. Need help?"

"I would love your help." I slid my hand up her leg. "Do you think we'll get much done?"

She splashed me with water, then got out of the tub. I watched her walk, stark naked and dripping wet, across the deck as she went to retrieve the towels from the armoire. She was fucking gorgeous and I couldn't believe she was here. She walked back and stood over me, holding out my towel. I got up and out of the tub, water cascading off my body, and took it.

"Thanks," I said, wrapping it around my waist. "You hungry?"

She shook her head.

"Couldn't eat a bite. The adrenaline is starting to wear off and I think I'm about ready to crash," she said.

"Here?" I asked hopefully.

"Here."

I smiled and took her hand. We started walking towards the back door.

"Then we should go upstairs. I've got a surprise for you."

She stopped and looked at me.

"Oh yeah? What's that?"

I wiggled my eyebrows at her.

"I happen to have a box of condoms upstairs."

A look passed through her eyes that struck me to the core. It was pure desire. For me.

"Funny," she said, slipping out of the towel. "Suddenly, I'm not so tired anymore."

CHAPTER TWENTY-ONE

Bree

Well. That whole evening took an unexpected turn. I rolled over in bed, staring at Dave's silent, sleeping form. He was lying on his stomach, sheets gathered around his waist. His arms were raised above his head and his hair was fanned out across the pillow. I reached over and gently wound a strand around my finger and smiled. That hair felt fucking great across my tits. He sighed in his sleep and I released him, pushing back the blankets and getting out of bed.

I picked up my phone to check the time. Seven a.m. I glanced back at Dave, hesitant to wake him but also knowing he had a store to open. I was trying to figure out how long it would take him to get ready and how much longer I could let him sleep when one eye popped open and he smiled up at me.

"Good morning," he murmured.

I walked around to his side of the bed, bent down, and kissed him on the mouth.

"Good morning, yourself."

I walked over to his dresser and opened a few drawers, rummaging around until I found a pair of his boxer briefs and a T-shirt, both of which I slipped on.

"Make yourself at home," he said, a smile in his voice.

I turned to face him, fully aware of the effect seeing me in his clothes would have on him.

"Does this bother you?" I asked, batting my eyelashes.

He pulled down the sheets to show me just how much it didn't bother him.

*

By the time I got to work that evening, I'd napped, showered, eaten, and relived the previous night's adventures a hundred times in my head. Every time I thought about Dave, a shiver went through me and I was forced to clamp my thighs together.

I couldn't believe I'd been so stupid. It was obvious from the first kiss that sex between us would be mind-blowing. I glanced down the bar at the middle-aged men in their suits and ties and wondered if any of them would've been able to take me to the places Dave had taken me in bed. To date, none of them had satisfied me like he had. I had stayed away from guys like Dave for so long I'd forgotten what it could be like, to be intimate with someone who truly enjoyed someone else's body rather than just seeking out pleasure for their own.

And I had had as much fun exploring his body as he'd had with mine. And while I hated to admit it, there was something about his level of fitness and stamina that just, well, shut the suits out of his league altogether. Had I really been so materialistic to place wealth and security over the incredible feelings coursing through my body at that moment?

And then I paused. Maybe it was the hormones making me forget sense. I shook off the thought, not ready to let go of my post-coital glow.

"You look like you're having an entire conversation with yourself," Jen said, laughing.

I looked over at her. She was beside me behind the bar, stacking the clean glasses out of the dishwasher. I hadn't even heard her come in. I offered a weak smile.

"No, no, no. You can't fool me. I'm the one that saw you come out of that bathroom last night, remember? I also saw you sneak out back after everyone was good and drunk. Spill."

I couldn't stop the smile that broke out across my face if I tried. I glanced around, but all the customers were gathered at the other end of the bar and dinner service hadn't started yet. I told Jen the whole story.

"Well, look at that. And how do you feel about him?" she asked.

"I don't know. I like him. I really do. I mean, we were friends, and that was great, but Jen? This is soooo much better."

She laughed so loud a few patrons looked up from their drinks. Adam caught her eye and signalled it was time to return to her duties. She pulled off her apron and put it under the bar.

"I'm happy for you, I am. I think this is a much better fit for you than—" she waved her arm towards the suits.

I rolled my eyes.

"Listen, my dating preferences—"

"Are irrelevant now. Have a great shift, Bree. I'm sure tonight will be even better than last night. Well, work-wise, at least." She grinned as she walked away, shaking her head.

*

I struck a deal with Adam and took Thursday off to help Dave with the move. He never would've gone for it, being the first week of the new menu, but I had a secret weapon—Jen. As soon as she overheard me talking to him, she walked right over and said she'd be happy to take my shift, and that she knew the drink menu like the back of her hand. And then she slapped Adam lightly across the face with that hand and walked away.

"Well," he said. "I guess that's decided."

"When did she become your boss?" I asked, chuckling.

"Hey. She just got you the day off. I'd be careful if I were you." He gave me the eye then walked away.

Normally, I'd have taken advantage of a day off to sleep in, but given the move, I was up by seven. The move plus the fact I hadn't seen Dave since Wednesday morning. It had only been twenty-four hours but my entire body was screaming for him.

I pulled on a pair of shorts and a T-shirt, ate a bowl of cereal over the sink, then took off for the record shop. By the time I got there, the moving truck was already loading the first of the boxes. Dave saw me on the sidewalk and came over, planting a kiss on my forehead.

"Not good enough," I said.

He grinned and bent down to give me a proper kiss.

"I'm sorry I'm late," I murmured.

"Not late. I'm just getting an early start. I need your help on the other side."

He wrapped an arm around my waist and I lay my head on his shoulder. In the distance, we both saw Chris rounding the corner as he approached the shop. He broke out into a smile when he saw the two of us.

"He knew?" I asked Dave, incredulous.

"We spend a lot of time together," he said.

I reached up and kissed Dave's cheek. Chris averted his eyes as he came to a stop beside us and watched the movers.

"Good morning, Chris," I said.

He bobbed his head shyly.

"Hey, Chris," Dave said charitably, "why don't you go ask the movers how long they think it'll take to load up?"

Chris looked relieved as he left us and ambled over to the moving truck. Dave squeezed my waist and I looked up at him.

"What?" I asked.

"What's going on here?" he asked.

I looked around.

"I think you're moving," I said.

"That's not what I meant."

I took a step away from him, glanced at the truck, then considered him carefully.

"Do you really want to have a relationship conversation two days after we slept together AND on your moving day?"

He looked positively lost.

"I just want to know where we stand. It's been two days for you, but it's been months over here," he reminded me.

I reached over and stroked his cheek, letting my hand fall to his shoulder where I played with the ends of his hair.

"I'm standing right here, next to you. Can that be enough for now?"

His arm snaked around me again and he drew me close, kissing me thoroughly before responding.

"Yes."

CHAPTER TWENTY-TWO

Dave

It turns out it made no difference what Bree thought or said. Within twenty-four hours, the entire town of Mountain Valley had decided we were in a relationship. She certainly didn't quell the rumours. The woman was unable to keep her hands off me. I wasn't complaining.

It was hard for us to find time to spend together for the first couple of weeks. She was crazy busy at work and I was all tied up with the move. Whenever either of us had a free moment, we spent it together. We'd made use of Cagney's restroom three more times over those two weeks, the bookshop/record store not being a viable option.

"How's it going at the new location?" Bree asked one evening, pulling up the straps of her dress.

I checked my reflection in the bathroom mirror, grabbing a few tissues from the box on the counter and handing them to her to clean up. She took one and wiped the corner of her mouth, grinning sheepishly. I kissed her quickly.

"It's going okay. Isabelle takes some getting used to, but we'll work it out." I looked around. "They're going to figure us out one of these days, you know. Adam's not an idiot."

"I know," she said. "Liam's given me the side-eye a couple of times already."

"Please. Like he hasn't done the same?"

Bree backed away from the counter as if the thought had just occurred to her.

"Really?" I said. "You never stopped to think you weren't the only one doing this?"

She shuddered.

"I just kind of assumed he'd use the walk-in," she said.

"Okay. That's definitely TMI. I eat here, remember?"

She giggled and picked up my shirt, handing it to me so I could pull it over my head.

"You don't giggle often," I remarked. "I like it."

She turned around and reapplied her lipstick, then turned and ran her fingers through my hair.

"I've got to get back to work. What's your plan? You going to stick around?"

"I don't think so. I'm going to head back to the store. I got some new inventory this morning I didn't have a chance to unpack and the new sign is being delivered tomorrow."

"What did you settle on?" she asked.

"Mountain Valley Records and Books. Original, huh?"

"It works," she said. "I like it."

"Listen," I said. "This is getting ridiculous. We need to find a way to spend more time together."

"Can't you get Chris to cover for you during the day? You're paying him now, aren't you?"

"I am, but he's helping Mrs. F. get organized. This was a big upheaval for her and we've got to treat the whole thing with kid gloves. We're still doing the festival, right?"

She took my face in her hands and kissed me gently.

"Absolutely. It's just a few more days away. We've got three-day passes. It will be amazing."

She stopped, a puzzled look crossing her face.

"What's wrong?" I asked, sensing doom.

She shook her head, waving me off.

"Nothing. I forgot I had a doctor's appointment on Friday morning. Shitty timing, but they're impossible to change. But things don't get started until afternoon, right?"

"First show on our list is at three," I confirmed.

She kissed me again, a little longer this time.

"I will be there. I got the entire weekend off."

I stared at her, impressed.

"How'd you manage that?"

"It was brilliant, actually. I spoke to Mason and he spoke to some of the band's managers. I lined up celebrity bartenders for the three days of the festival. Clears my schedule completely. Best part? Adam and Liam were blown away by the idea. The restaurant is booked solid the entire weekend."

"The record shop, the tasting menu, celebrity bartenders. You really know how to get shit done, don't you?"

She paused, about to say something, then closed her mouth.

"What is it?" I asked.

"Nothing. Really."

I studied her, then blew it off.

"I can't wait to fuck you behind the beer tent," I said, eliciting a blush and a smile.

"Bring condoms this time."

I rolled my eyes.

"That's getting pretty tenuous when it comes to public sex, don't you think?"

"And that brings us back to my doctor's appointment," she smiled. "I'm going to talk to her about options."

My dick stirred, despite the fact I'd just fucked her from behind over the sink.

"Okay," she said, bringing me back to planet Earth. "I'll catch you later. Call me."

She gave me another quick kiss and was out the door.

*

"I haven't seen your lady friend in a while," Mrs. Fairfax said.

She had just finished serving a customer and was sipping on a cup of tea watching me unpack the latest shipment of vinyl. Chris was practically foaming at the mouth as he saw the treasures coming out of the box.

"You're on salary now," I reminded him.

"I know, I know."

He couldn't help himself. He touched each album as it emerged: Pearl Jam, AC/DC, The

Rolling Stones, David Bowie—the kid was just over the moon.

"He reminds me of you," Mrs. F. said.

"Don't I know it," I laughed.

"So? Your lady friend?"

Isabelle Fairfax was nothing if not persistent.

"We've got opposite schedules. I work days, she works nights. It makes things a little challenging. Don't you worry. We're just fine."

She looked me up and down.

"You two even look alike, with your jeans, long hair, tattoos…"

"Yes, I get the picture."

In truth, there had never been two people more perfect for each other than the two of us. We were alike in so many ways—our determination, our ability to read people, our views on life. And yet different in all the right ways—her extrovert to my introvert, my rational to her passion. We could see each other's points of view and still act as each other's anchors. It was an intoxicating mix.

I looked up to see Isabelle still staring at me, a wistful look on her face.

"Yes?" I asked.

"I was just wondering why young people don't get married anymore. You must be in your thirties. You have no wife, no children. Don't you want children?"

"I do. Someday." I thought for a minute. "I guess sooner than I thought, given the whole 'thirties' thing. But I think my generation is more into living for the moment than the future. You grew up imagining where you wanted to be at the end of the journey. I'm just enjoying the ride."

"And your lady friend?"

"Bree and I are on the same page. She's not in any rush to get anywhere, either. In fact, I'd bet I'm more committed than she is."

Chris snorted in the background and I turned to find him amongst the stacks.

"You have something to say?" I asked.

"You don't see the goofy expressions on your face all day," he smirked. "You are definitely more in love."

I started.

"I didn't say anything about love."

Both Chris and Isabelle burst out laughing at that.

"What? What's so funny?" I demanded.

Isabelle just took another sip of tea while Chris returned to filing away the new albums in their respective bins. I glowered at both of them, then pulled out my phone to text Bree. It had been at least an hour since we'd last spoken.

*

On Thursday night I tried to lure Bree over after work with the promise of an outdoor soak after a hard week, but she turned me down. She insisted on getting home and getting a good night's sleep before the weekend's crazy schedule kicked in. This festival was the highlight of the summer, and the town was overrun with tourists.

Chris had volunteered to take over the shop for the duration of the weekend. There were a few bands he wanted to see, but they were playing at night. As a thank you, I bought him the passes. I'd heard from his mother twice over the past few weeks, thanking me profusely for helping him turn things around.

Friday felt like light-years away. I was like a kid on Christmas eve, getting into bed early on Thursday night with the hopes it would make morning come faster. I tossed and turned for an hour before heading outside, drawing a bath, and lighting a joint. It was a pleasant diversion from trying to sleep, but it did nothing to take my mind of Bree. Every time I even looked at the tub all I could do was picture her naked in it, soap suds swirling around her breasts as they peaked from the surface of the water.

I grew hard at the thought and cursed myself, then shrugged it off and realized there were worse ways to pass the time.

CHAPTER TWENTY-THREE

Bree

"So. What can I do for you today, Bree?"

I looked up at the doctor and smiled. I was lying on her exam table, naked save for a paper cloth, with my feet up in stirrups, and she wanted to know what she could do? Maybe restore a little of my dignity?

"I was hoping to talk to you about birth control," I said.

She poked and prodded a little inside while feeling my abdomen with her other hand.

"Hmm," she said. "Any idea what form?"

"Well, since I'm in my thirties now, I'm thinking not the pill. What about an IUD?"

Dr. Jamison removed her hand and took a step back, studying me.

"Are you in a relationship?" she asked.

"Is that relevant?" I countered.

She nodded curtly and took off her gloves, disposing of them in a nearby trashcan.

"Get dressed, come into my office, and we'll talk."

I did as told and a few minutes later found myself seated across the desk from her. She was looking over my file and glanced up as I sat down.

"There are a few options we can discuss. First of all, you're sure you're not pregnant?" she asked.

"Positive," I said.

"Date of your last period?"

"July 11," I answered.

She looked up.

"It's August 15," she said. "You're a week late."

I started.

"Am I?"

I hadn't even noticed. Between the restaurant, the record shop move, the constant sex with Dave—it had just never occurred to me. Dr. Jamison reached into her desk and pulled out a urine specimen container and handed it to me.

"Why don't you go pee? We'll clear this up right away."

I reluctantly took the jar from her, making my way slowly to the bathroom. *How could I be pregnant?* I walked into the bathroom and locked the door behind me. I put the jar down on the counter, pulled down my pants, and sat down on the toilet.

And then it hit me. That first time. We hadn't used a condom. But I'd *just* finished my period. There was no way I was fertile then. This had to be a mistake. Stress from the launch. Of course that's what it was.

I closed the bottle and washed my hands, preparing to return to the doctor. When I arrived back in her office, she was on the phone and gave me the "hold on" signal. I smiled and sat. When she hung up, I passed her the bottle and she took out a pregnancy test, dipping it inside. Then she set the whole thing aside.

"We'll do this old school," she said, smiling. "If it's positive, we'll follow it up with a blood test, okay?"

I nodded, frozen to the seat. She started talking to me about IUDs, but I couldn't focus on a thing she said. I was staring at the test, sitting there on the corner of her desk, the result window just out of sight. I glanced up at the clock and watched the second hand move ever-so-slowly around its face.

"So, what do you think?" she asked.

I snapped back to attention, turning to her. My face must have been blank because she offered a sympathetic smile.

"I was asking if you'd prefer an IUD with or without hormones? There are advantages and disadvantages to consider."

The timer on her phone went off and she flashed me a smile. She reached over and picked up the test. I didn't need my psych degree or years behind the bar to read the expression on her face. I was pregnant. She looked up at me cautiously.

"Might it be a false positive?" I asked.

"That's why we'll do the blood test. I assume this wasn't planned?" she asked gently.

"No, it most definitely was not."

I stood up and started pacing, then sat down again.

"Do you need a moment alone?" she asked.

I smiled gratefully at her.

"No, that's okay." I checked the time again, this time actually seeing it. "There's somewhere I've got to be. Thank you, Doctor."

She nodded.

"Stop and see the nurse on your way out. She'll draw the blood for you and I'll call you first thing Monday morning when I have the results. Until then, don't—"

I held up my hand to silence her, and she acquiesced. I turned and left her office.

*

I met Dave just outside the festival grounds. He was standing by the ticket booth talking to Katie and Jax. As soon as I walked up, he wrapped his arm around my waist and pulled me in close, giving me a kiss on the cheek before turning back to his conversation.

I hadn't seen him in a couple of days. I should've been thrilled. My skin should have been sizzling at his touch. But all I felt was cold, like there was ice water flowing through my veins. I glanced over at him, then at Katie and Jax, but I couldn't seem to follow the conversation.

It had been a mistake coming to the festival, but I'd had no choice. I had three days to kill before the doctor called. I already made a silent vow not to spend the weekend taking pregnancy tests every hour, so what else was there to do? I'd listen to kick-ass music from some of my favourite bands and fuck my boyfriend like there was no tomorrow.

Because maybe there was no tomorrow.

"Hey? You ready?" Dave was eyeing me, so I gave him a quick smile and squeezed the hand on my waist.

"Absolutely," I said. "Let's do this."

The four of us passed through the ticket booth, showing our passes and making our way to the main stage. As Jax and Katie threw a blanket down on the ground, Dave pulled my hand to follow him.

"Come with me to the beer tent," he said.

"Already?" I asked.

He laughed.

"That's not what I meant, but sure, I'm game." He waggled his eyebrows at me and I couldn't help but laugh.

"Keep it in your pants, mister."

We walked over to the tent and Dave ordered four beers. I grabbed a few bags of chips and threw them in. We walked back to where Katie and Jax had set up.

"Anyone else joining us?" I asked.

"Chance and Tess are working at the moment. We're switching off shifts. Summer help has been a bitch this year. Mason's shooting but is going to try to come by tonight."

"Anyone heard from Lainey and Logan lately?" Jax asked.

Katie turned to him.

"They may swing through tomorrow," she said.

Dave passed me a beer and I brought it to my lips and paused. I glanced around and while no one was looking, lowered the cup again. My plan for the day had been to get buzzed and listen to great music. It looked like the first part of that plan was off the table. While everyone was drinking and talking, I set my cup on the grass beside me and tipped it casually, letting a slow but constant stream pour out.

The grounds filled up quickly with people and before long, sounds were starting to come from the stage. We all got up, feeling the anticipation build as the first act stepped up and picked up their instruments. The crowd went wild as the music started and Dave reached over to squeeze my hand. I looked over at him and smiled, but inside, all I felt was panic.

I was pregnant. I knew it. What the fuck was I going to do?

*

Three hours and four acts into the festival, the late afternoon sun was beating down on my head, and because everyone thought I was drinking beer, I was severely dehydrated. My head was pounding and my stomach was starting to churn. I licked my lips and looked around for Dave.

I spotted him a few feet over, laughing with Toni. I hadn't even seen her arrive. I raised my hand to signal to her, but she didn't notice, too wrapped up in conversation. The next band was setting up and I didn't think I would make it another five minutes without water.

"Dave," I squeaked.

Nothing.

I left our spot and walked over to where he was, tugging on the back of his shirt. He turned to me, the smile dropping from his face as he took me in.

"Bree! What's the matter?" he asked.

"Nothing," I said, shaking my head. "Just need water."

I looked over at Toni and saw the alarm in her eyes. I glanced down at myself to see if maybe I'd missed something.

"What's wrong?" I asked.

"You look like the walking dead," Toni said, taking my arm. "Let's go find somewhere for you to sit."

"Don't be ridiculous," I said, shaking her loose. "I just need some water. Dave—"

I turned towards him a smidge too fast and the entire world blurred out of focus. I reached out for him, but he was just out of my grasp. The last thing I remembered was the feeling that I was falling through clouds.

*

"Bree! Bree! BREE!"

Dave was shouting. Why was Dave shouting? I tried to open my eyes to tell him to shut up, but it proved harder than I'd anticipated.

"Be quiet, Dave, that's not helping."

That was Toni. That was better.

"Go get the paramedics. They're at the first aid table. Go."

I heard Dave shuffle off as Katie and Jax chattered in the background. The light behind my eyes turned dark as Toni knelt to whisper in my ear.

"Bree? Honey? Are you okay?"

I managed to get one eye open and I looked at her. I was lying on the grass, people milling all around and staring at me. I closed my eye again.

"Oh shit," I said. "How fucking embarrassing. Can you make them all go away?"

"I'm afraid not," she said. "And I think it's about to get worse."

"Excuse me, Excuse me, coming through."

Two loud male voices boomed above the crowd and I forced both eyes open in time to see them coming towards me with a stretcher. I sat up and pointed.

"I do not need that," I said firmly.

Dave appeared out of nowhere and knelt beside me. Toni stood and let him take over. I wished she hadn't.

"You will do whatever they tell you. Are you okay? What happened?" he asked, concerned.

"I'm fine. Too much beer. Too much sun. Too many long hours at the restaurant. I'll be fine." I looked up at the paramedics as I got to my feet. "I'm fine, really. I can stand, I can walk."

I took a few steps to demonstrate, trying a curtsy at the end and wobbling a little. Dave reached for my elbow and as much as I wanted to shake him off, I needed him to steady me.

"All right," one of the paramedics conceded. "But you should really head home, miss. A few more sets aren't worth it."

I nodded solemnly and the two guys took off with their stretcher. I smiled at Dave.

"I'll make my way home, you stay," I said.

"Are you crazy? I'm going with you," he said, gathering his things.

Toni stepped over and put her hand on Dave's arm.

"Hey. I've got to switch off with Liam anyway. Let me take her home. We'll be fine. You stay."

CHAPTER TWENTY-FOUR

Dave

I watched Bree and Toni leave the festival grounds with an uneasy feeling. Why had I let her leave like that? Why hadn't I insisted on going?

"There's nothing you can do," Katie said, reading my mind. "When a woman makes up her mind, that's it."

I turned to her and smiled.

"Okay, shut up," Jax said as the next band was introduced.

Once again, the crowd went wild and within moments, I was swept up in the music. I felt awful about Bree, but she'd be fine. I'd swing by after the last act and make sure she was okay, or maybe even see if she wanted me to stay over.

It had been a while since I'd been to a show and nothing fed my soul like live music. No one played Mountain Valley. Closest we got was the resort town a half-hour down the highway. I'd seen maybe two shows over the past year and I'd planned to take full advantage of the weekend. But I'd wanted Bree by my side. Every once in a while, I glanced over to where she should have been and felt a knot in my gut.

*

It was past midnight when I got home. I thought about calling Bree, but I didn't want to wake her. And we were way too early in the relationship for a surprise late-night visit.

But as soon as I awoke Saturday morning, I jumped in the shower, dressed, and headed out my front door. It was about nine when I arrived at her place. I saw a car parked out front and I knew Nick was out on a road trip with Desi. They were bringing a load of furniture out to Lainey's dad, Colm, in BC. I figured someone was with Bree. That was good.

I got out of the car and grabbed the flowers I'd thought to pick up, then rang her bell. When the buzzer went, I raced up the stairs, only to find Jen grabbing her bag on the way out. Bree was standing next to her, in pajamas and a fuzzy robe, not looking her absolute best. I walked right over and gave her a kiss. Jen glanced at her.

"Toni will be here in around ten minutes. You want me to wait?" she asked.

"No, it's fine. Dave's here," Bree said, looking at me pointedly.

Jen looked between us and nodded. Bree turned to go sit on the couch and Jen pulled me aside.

"She's not feeling great. I think she's just exhausted. Don't stay too long," she said.

I bit my lip and nodded. I really wanted to say I'd stay as long as I fucking wanted, but I sensed that wasn't the wisest move. I watched her go down the stairs then shut the door. I joined Bree on the couch.

"You okay?" I asked. "I was really worried about you."

She gave me a weak smile.

"I'll be fine. Too much sun. Too much beer. You know the drill. But I think you should go without me today."

"Fuck that. I'll stay here with you. Nowhere else I'd rather be."

She chewed her bottom lip.

"Dave, really, you should go. This is once a year and I know how much you were looking forward to it. I'll just be sleeping anyway. And I'll join you tomorrow. I'm sure I'll be fine by then. Maybe even tonight."

I turned to face her, studying her unreadable expression.

"What's up, Bree?" I asked.

"Nothing is up. Why do you have to assume something's up? I just don't feel well. Isn't that enough?"

I shrunk back, stunned. I'd never heard that tone from her before. There was definitely something up.

"Listen," I said. "If we're going to do this thing, I should be here for the ugly, too."

"Do what thing, Dave?"

Again I cringed.

"Um, this thing that we're doing? Dating? A relationship? I'm sorry, where have you been these past few weeks?" I asked.

She stood up and walked to the other end of the living room. Leaning against the wall she looked over at me, assessing me.

"I've been right here, with you. And I've been having a great time. But really, where is it all leading?"

"Where is this coming from?" I asked.

"I mean, what are your plans in life, Dave Winter?"

"My plans? I own a record shop, a great house, and I have the world's best girlfriend. I'm good."

"That's enough for you?"

"Yes." I stared at her, realization dawning. "But that's not enough for you."

I stood up slowly.

"You want greater things." I realized I was still clutching the flowers and put them down on the couch. "You want someone who can give you greater things."

I nodded to myself as I walked towards the door. I reached for the handle but the door opened before I had the chance. Toni walked in, surveyed the scene, and started backing out.

"I'm just leaving," I said.

"Everything okay?" she asked.

"Not a damn clue."

I turned back to look at Bree, still leaning up against the wall. But the weirdest shade of green had passed across her face. I turned to Toni.

"You may want to help your friend. She's not looking so great."

And I walked out the door.

CHAPTER TWENTY-FIVE

Bree

"You didn't tell him."

"You're lucky I told you," I said.

Toni stood in the doorway, watching Dave's form retreating down the stairs. She closed the door gently and turned to me.

"You have to tell him," she said.

"I do not. First of all, I don't know anything for sure." Toni just stared at me. "Second of all, I haven't decided what to do yet."

She went and sat down on the couch.

"Come sit down. Dave was right. You're not looking so great."

"I think I have to puke."

As soon as the words were out of my mouth, the bile was rising in my throat. I turned and made a beeline for the bathroom, getting there just in time. I washed up and gargled with mouthwash before returning to Toni.

"I guess I can scratch morning sickness off the list," I said.

"It doesn't only happen once," she said.

"Fuck."

I sat down heavily on the couch next to her, laying my head on her shoulder. She stroked my hair, mumbling some soothing words that did nothing for me but seemed to soothe her so I let her carry on.

"Why won't you tell him?" she asked softly.

"Because if I tell him before I've decided what to do, he'll feel pressured to be excited about a baby and we barely even know each other. And he's not father material."

"Excuse me? Dave Winter is not father material? What on God's green earth makes you say that?"

"Look at him. He has zero ambition. He's going to be happy running that record shop for the rest of his life."

"So what?"

"No. Any children I have will be cared for. No precarious finances. No housing insecurity—"

"Housing insecurity? Dave owns a beautiful home. What the fuck are you talking about, Bree?"

I stood up again and shook my head fiercely.

"No. If I decide to have this child, I will find a suitable father. I'm early enough."

"You would deceive a man into thinking someone else's child is his?" Toni asked, incredulous.

"Of course not! I just mean I'm not visibly pregnant. I can still get dates. Once they fall for me…"

Toni stood up and shook her head, then walked over to me and draped an arm over my shoulder.

"I think the hormones are already fucking you up, sweetheart. Please don't repeat any of what you just said to anyone else. And please do not pursue that plan any longer. I think you should give yourself some time, some space, and you'll make the right call."

I smiled at her, unsure.

"You think?"

"I do. Now go get some rest."

*

I was alone Monday morning when the call came in. Toni and Jen had taken shifts with me all weekend, but when Sunday night rolled around I insisted they go out and enjoy their time off. Mondays were sacred to Cagney's staff. We rarely even interacted with each other.

I'd skipped the rest of the festival. I'd noticed I felt better in the afternoons, but I didn't want to risk seeing Dave. I was hoping to stay off his radar until I sorted things out.

When I picked up my phone and saw No Caller ID, I knew who it was.

"Hello?" I said.

"Good morning, Bree. It's Dr. Jamison."

"I'm pregnant."

"Well, I'd prefer if you came into the office this morning."

"I'm not coming into the office. I know I'm pregnant. Can you just confirm that for me, please?"

"And what makes you so certain?" she asked.

"I've been puking all weekend?"

I heard her sigh through the phone.

"Yes, you're pregnant. But you'll still need to come in. We have to discuss your plans, your care—"

"Yeah, I got it. I will call the receptionist and book something for this week. That good?"

"Very good. I'll see you this week, Bree. Take care of yourself."

I put the phone back down on the night table and rolled over onto my back. Staring up at the ceiling, for the first time, I let my hand wander over to my belly. My palm pressed flat against the skin, I tried to see if I could feel anything, but of course, it was too early.

But at that moment, I knew I was having the baby.

*

When I showed up for my shift on Tuesday night, I headed straight for the kitchen. I was starving. As I swung through the doors, the smells of that night's menu wafted up to greet me and I almost started salivating. I most certainly felt woozy.

Liam and Toni looked up when I walked in— Liam with a smile and Toni with a look of mild surprise and concern. I shot her a warning look and wandered over to check out the various pots and pans.

"I've already made you a plate," Liam said, pointing to the back table.

I smiled and sauntered over, picking it up and diving in. Seafood pasta, one of my favourites.

"This is fucking delicious," I said between mouthfuls.

Liam smiled and saluted. Toni walked over and peered into my bowl, already half empty.

"Maybe slow down a little?" she suggested.

I looked up at her and smiled, biting off the ends of my noodles and letting them drop in the bowl. I was being a pig. I placed the bowl down on the table and turned to Liam.

"So, things back to normal this week?" I asked.

"Yup, but that was quite a rush, wasn't it?" he smiled.

"Sure was, Chef. Thank you for that."

He shook his head.

"You knocked it out of the park. The bar made so much money last week Adam's been laughing all day."

I turned to Toni.

"It's you and me, tonight?" I asked.

"Yup." She glanced over at Liam. "He's got a hot date."

Liam dropped a kiss on Toni's head then pulled off his apron, tossing it in the hamper set up in the corner.

"Have a great night, ladies. See you tomorrow."

As soon as he was gone, Toni turned back to me.

"How are you?"

"I'm fine. Really. I spoke to the doctor yesterday. It's official. And I'm going to keep it."

Toni pulled me in for a hug and I gave myself over to her completely. I hadn't realized how much stress had built up over the weekend until I let someone else take some of it on for me. That's what friends were all about. She held on longer than necessary, then pulled back smiled warmly.

"I'm here for you. And so is Jen. Neither of us will say a word until you're ready. We'll do this together."

I smiled.

"I haven't given up hope on a suit."

The smile dropped from Toni's face.

"Bree."

"Don't Bree me. I've thought about this. I know what it's like to have nothing. I don't want that for my kid."

She sucked in her breath and I could tell she was biting her lip. I didn't care. I didn't want to hear what she had to say anyway. I shrugged my shoulders and walked out of the kitchen. It was time to set up the bar and get to work.

*

The week went on, busier than usual with the tourists who'd opted to hang out and vacation for a while after the festival. Mornings were awful, and every time I bent over the toilet I thanked the employment gods I worked a night shift. By noon, it was like everything was just fine and dandy. Except I couldn't cram enough food down my throat.

I met with the doctor on Thursday. I told her I planned to keep the baby and she walked me through what to expect over the next nine months. It was a little overwhelming, and it must have shown because she asked if I'd prefer to return with the father.

"I'm not sure the father will be in the picture," I said.

She tactfully looked down.

"I see. Okay, then, feel free to bring a friend to your appointments. It's often better to have someone with you."

"Thanks," I said. "I'll do that."

We set up my first appointment for a month later and after a lecture about proper nutrition and sleep hygiene, I was off.

By the time Friday night rolled around, I was starting to show signs of wear. I glanced over from behind the busy bar and saw Jen whispering in Adam's ear, and him nodding. Moments later, she was by my side pulling on an apron.

"I'm not leaving," I said.

"I'm not letting you. I'm just pitching in."

I threw her a smile and a dish towel and moved down the bar to see who needed drinks. I stopped a few times on my way to the other end, getting beers and mixing cocktails. By the time I worked the length, Jake had come in and taken a seat at the far end. I smiled as I approached.

"What can I get you, Jake? Or is it bartender's choice?" I asked.

He smiled.

"Bartender's choice. Definitely." He paused, so I waited before turning away. "Listen, I don't want you to think I'm here because of you. I mean, I'm here because you make a great drink, but I heard what you said."

I smiled, then leaned across the bar and kissed his cheek.

"Thank you," I whispered in his ear.

As I turned away to select the bottles, I once again cursed myself for not giving it more of a chance with Jake. My hand went unconsciously to my belly and I gave it a little rub. *What would be best for her?* I realized that was how I had to think from that point on. I took a deep breath and turned to hand Jake his drink.

"Here you go. On the house."

He took a sip and a slow smile spread across his face.

"Delicious. Marry me," he said.

I laughed and swatted him across the shoulder, then turned to see Dave standing at the other end of the bar.

CHAPTER TWENTY-SIX

Dave

I stood there, watching Bree flirt with Jake as my blood pressure rose. I tried not to jump to any conclusions. Mainly because Jen had just leaned across the bar and told me not to jump to any conclusions. But it was pretty fucking hard.

We hadn't spoken all week. I figured she wasn't feeling well, was going through some shit, and needed her space. I did not realize we were flirting with other people. I balled my hands into fists, thrusting them in my lap as Bree made her way over.

"Hey," she said.

"Hey."

"You want a beer?"

I glanced across the bar at Jake, then back at her. There was no point in being mad. I knew who she was the moment I met her. She tried to warn me time and again.

"Sure," I said.

She grabbed a mug and filled it for me but I saw her expression grow serious as Jake called to her from the other end of the bar. She looked at me, unable to conceal the guilt.

"What's going on over there?" I asked.

"We need to talk, Dave."

I sat up straighter.

"Are you and him—?"

"No! Nothing like that. I promise. But can you...stick around?"

"I'm not going anywhere," I said, glaring at the fucking suit.

Bree went down the bar to refill Jake's glass.

"Bree," Jen called. "Can you grab a few more bottles of the burgundy from the wine cellar?"

Bree nodded and took off for the back of the restaurant. Then Jen looked up and smiled at me.

"All good?" she asked.

"All good with me. All good with her?" I asked, nodding after Bree.

Jen watched her retreating back and then turned back to me. She pulled her towel from the waist of her apron and started wiping glasses dry as she pulled them from the dish-washer before putting them away.

"Give her a little time, Dave. Be patient."

"You want to tell me what's going on?" I asked.

"No. I think I gave you enough." She smiled sweetly, then took two dirty glasses and headed down the bar, dropping them in the sink.

*

I slipped off my stool and headed down the hallway after Bree. Fuck that shit. There was definitely something going on and I wanted to know what it was.

I made my way down the stairs and pushed open the door to the wine cellar. It was a small room, all the walls lined with specially-designed wine holders. There must have been over two hundred bottles in the room. It was quite the sight.

Bree was in the corner, reaching for a bottle just out of grasp.

"Let me get that," I said.

I was standing right behind her and she turned her head to look at me. I reached up across her body to pull down the bottle she was after. I handed it to her, her back now pressed against my chest. Her breathing was erratic and mine wasn't far behind.

"Here," I mumbled.

"Thanks," she breathed.

The heat coming off her was insane. Who was this woman? She was running hot and cold, flirting with other men—this was not the Bree I knew.

She turned around and put the bottle down on the floor before reaching up and running the side of her hand along my cheek.

On the other hand, this Bree wasn't so bad.

"What are you doing?" I asked.

"I assume you followed me down here for a reason," she whispered.

She traced a line down my neck across my chest, down my stomach, and heading towards my belt. I put my hand on her wrist to stop her.

"Bree. What's going on with you? First, you kick me out of your apartment, then I catch you flirting with Jake, now you're coming on to me after telling me you had something serious to discuss? What the hell?"

She put her finger against my lips, then replaced it with her mouth. A million thoughts went through my mind, but the one that won out was, *screw it*. I gathered her in my arms and kissed her long and well. She pulled away and turned the lock on the door. Then, grinning, she stripped off her jeans and tank top, leaving her in nothing but her bra and panties.

Mesmerized, I reached out and hooked my thumbs into her the sides of her panties, lowering them as I dropped to my knees before her, planting a kiss on my very favourite spot on earth. She put her hands on my shoulder and squeezed.

"Get up here," she said.

I obeyed at once, rising to my feet and taking her face in my hands, covering her mouth with mine. She yielded easily, welcoming me as I deepened the kiss. She pressed up against me and started to grind. I groaned, my cock so hard it was pressing against the zipper of my jeans.

She reached down and undid my belt, pushing my jeans down and freeing me from my boxer briefs. She wrapped her hand around me and started stroking, slowly but firmly.

"Fuck," I muttered, pushing her up against the wall.

The bottles shook, threatening to fall. She put a hand on my chest.

"Gently," she whispered.

I pushed down the cups of her bra, exposing her breasts. Her nipples were at attention, and I lowered my head, tracing a circle around one before coaxing it into my mouth. I nibbled gently until I elicited the noises I was now hearing in my sleep. I slipped a hand between her legs, finding her so ready my cock grew another inch.

She reached down and took hold of me, guiding me towards her.

"I have a condom in my pocket," I mumbled, reaching back. She put out a hand to stop me.

"I saw the doctor, remember?"

"You took care of it?" I asked, wanting to be sure there was no misunderstanding.

"It's taken care of," she assured me as she slipped me inside.

"Oh, fuck, Bree."

We stayed like that for a moment, her pressed up against the bottles, me holding onto the shelf behind her head. I started to move.

"Oh, Dave. Oh, god, yes," she moaned as I fucked her slowly.

Every time I went above a snail's pace, the bottles would shake. Her hands moved to my hips, then my ass, as she clutched me tightly. The pace was agonizing and erotic all at once. The build was excruciating.

"Touch me," she begged.

I reached down between us and found her clit, rubbing small circles with my thumb as her head dropped back against the shelf. I leaned over and kissed her neck, making a path down to her breast. Keeping the same slow pace with my thrusts, I increased the rhythm with my thumb, and before long she was panting in my ear.

"Oh, yes, just like that, oh, fuck, I'm going to come," she cried.

One of her hands flew up to her mouth to cover her cries and I watched her as she came all over my cock. She let go of my ass completely, reaching down between us to squeeze my balls and I let go of the shelf, grabbing her shoulder as my orgasm ripped through me.

She leaned up and kissed me as I was coming down, and we held each other, motionless against the bottles of wine.

After what seemed like an eternity, she raised her head off my chest.

"I've got to get back to work," she said.

I laughed.

"Seriously?" I asked.

"Seriously."

CHAPTER TWENTY-SEVEN

Bree

Jen took one look at me as I took my place behind the bar and put away the bottles. She shook her head, a disgusted look on her face.

"Did you at least tell him?" she asked.

I looked down at my apron, suddenly having trouble tying it.

"So why did you fuck him in the wine cellar?" she persisted.

I looked up, sheepish.

"Because I'm really fucking horny?" I offered.

She let out a long, low sigh and glanced up at the clock.

"We've got an hour left until closing. Think you can keep it in your pants until then?"

I smiled and nodded. She shook her head once more and left me to serve my customers.

A few minutes later, Dave came back into the room. I caught Liam at the corner of the bar, taking note. He got off his stool and walked down towards me.

"Anything going on there?" Liam asked, nodding towards Dave.

"You know there's something going on there," I said.

"Right. Man, I knew he was the right one for you. So glad I gave you that push."

I looked at him like he was nuts.

"What are you talking about, Chef? You had nothing to do with this."

He just shrugged.

"If you say so. But I never had any intention of setting him up with Tammy."

My eyes must have gone like saucers. I glared at him, but he just laughed.

"Oh, come on, Bree. It all worked out in the end, right?"

I glanced over at Dave then down at my belly before looking at Liam again.

"We'll see."

*

Dave hung around until closing and then tried to convince me to go home with him. There was nothing I wanted more, my body still singing from our earlier encounter in the cellar. But the thought of waking up at his house in the morning was enough to stop me in my tracks. Unless I was ready to tell him about the pregnancy right there and then, there was no way I could mask the morning sickness that was sure to follow the next day.

"Come on, Bree. We barely see each other. Just come home with me."

We were leaving the restaurant and he was giving it one last try. I turned to him as we walked through the parking lot and put my hand on his shoulder.

"I'm exhausted. I just need sleep. If I go home with you, there will be no sleep," I said.

"I guess I can't argue with that," he grumbled.

I put my other hand on his other shoulder and leaned up to kiss him gently on the mouth. His arms went around me and we stayed there for a while, making out in the parking lot like a couple of teenagers.

"You sure?" he whispered.

"Positive."

I disentangled myself from his arms and gave him a last kiss on the cheek before unlocking my car and getting in.

"Are you okay to drive?" he asked.

"Haven't had a drop all night," I said.

I closed the door and he waved goodbye as I drove out of the lot. The entire drive home my body was screaming for his, reminding me once again of the incredible connection we'd forged in such a short time. Why hadn't I just told him?

I knew why. Dave wasn't equipped to be a father. He was a great guy, he'd be a fabulous boyfriend, but father wasn't a role I could picture him playing. He wanted different things in life. He didn't want to be tied to a job in order to support a family, and I didn't want to be the one to force him into that position. And I was completely unwilling to risk the stability in which I wanted—no, needed—to bring this child up. She would not go through the same things that I had. She would be taken care of.

By the time I got home, I resolved I was going to have to do one of two things—either come clean or make a clean break. What I was doing wasn't fair to either of us. By the time I got into bed, I still hadn't decided which it was going to be.

*

The doorbell rang at eight-thirty the next morning, waking me from a deep sleep. I cursed silently under my breath as I felt the first rumblings of unease grip my belly. I took a deep breath, grabbed a cracker from my bedside table, and rolled out of bed. I grabbed my robe and went to answer the door.

I figured it had to be Toni or Jen, both of whom had been checking up on me endlessly. I didn't even bother checking before hitting the buzzer, so I got what I deserved when Dave came up the stairs. I plastered a smile across my face and greeted him with a kiss on the cheek when he got to the landing.

"What are you doing here?" I asked.

He raised his hand, which was holding a bag from the deli. I could smell the bacon wafting up into the air and a wave of nausea rolled through me. I tried a smile and failed.

"I brought you breakfast..." he said, trailing off as I turned what must have been an odd shade of green. "Hey, are you okay?"

He put down the bag and reached out for me. I grabbed his wrist mid-air to stop him from touching me. I couldn't bear the idea of anything touching me. All I wanted was my toilet and the cool tile floor. I back away slowly.

"I'm fine," I mumbled.

"Bree, you are not fine. Look at you. You're green."

Not knowing what else to do, I slammed the door in his face as I took off down the hall for the bathroom. I made it just in time, hugging the porcelain as I prayed that maybe, just maybe, he'd have taken the hint and left.

"Bree? Where are you?"

No such luck.

I heard his voice coming down the hall, weaving in and out as he peered into the open doors along the way. Finally, he stopped outside the bathroom.

"Are you in there?"

"Yes."

"What the fuck is going on?"

"Nothing, I promise."

He tried the handle.

"Hey," I called. "A little early in the relationship for that, don't you think?"

I tried to make light of it, but it wasn't working. I could *hear* his concern through the closed door.

"Are you sick?" he asked.

"I might have a bug. I'm not sure. Why don't I call you later, when I'm feeling a little better?"

"I'm not going anywhere until I know you're okay."

Shit. I pulled my phone out of my bathrobe pocket and checked the time.

"You have to open the shop. You're going to be late."

I heard some mild cursing and a frustrated shuffle.

"Fine. You win. But I'll be back."

"Great. I'll see you later."

I slumped back against the wall and listened to his footsteps retreat, then the slam of the door.

*

I got to work early, knowing how busy it was on Saturday nights and wanting to make sure I got something to eat before my shift started.

I walked into the kitchen to find Toni, Jen, and Liam standing around Liam's workstation picking at the most delicious-looking chicken I'd ever seen. I floated over and poked my nose over Jen's shoulder. She looked at me and smiled as I reached in a pulled a piece of white meat off the breast.

"New recipe?" I asked.

Toni nodded as she reached for another piece. I didn't blame her. It was fucking unreal. I looked around for a plate so I could get myself a decent serving instead of picking with the vultures, and I felt Jen's eyes on me from behind.

"What is it?" I asked.

"You still haven't told him," she said.

"Told who what?" Liam asked, licking his fingers. "Great fucking job, Toni."

I turned in time to see Toni grinning ear to ear, loving Liam's praise. We were all like that with Liam. It took a lot to earn it, but when you did, he was so generous with it. He loved giving credit where it was due. More than that, he loved raising up each and every one of us who worked with him. He genuinely wanted to see us all succeed.

"Nothing," I said, glaring at Jen.

Toni walked over to the oven and pulled out a huge sheet pan and placed it on the workstation. It was two racks of ribs and I was salivating from the aroma alone.

"What, is it BBQ night and no one told me?" I asked.

"Just testing for future menus," Liam said. "You know the drill. Back to you, what's going on?"

Jen and Toni exchanged looks and then got really busy with their aprons. Liam just stared at me, giving me nowhere to go.

"Bree, when I was going through everything with Maggie, were you not all up in my shit? I thought we were a family here. What's up?"

At the mention of the word family, I burst into tears. His eyes widened and he rushed to my side, gathering me up in his arms. I had never had a family, I had never dared to dream of this crew as my family, yet there Liam was, dropping the word like it was a given that we were all bound together.

"Hey, hey, what's going on?" Liam asked, raising my chin with his finger.

I wiped my nose on my sleeve and pulled away from him. I looked over at the two women, but they just had those 'give it up already' looks on their faces. I sighed and turned back to Liam.

"I'm pregnant."

His jaw dropped like a cartoon. When he managed to pick it up off the floor, the craziest range of expressions passed through his eyes, from glee to concern to anger to a calm, neutral look.

"Congratulations," he said.

"Thank you," I smiled.

At that, he burst into a smile of his own and swept me up in his arms again.

"We can be happy about this? I'm so happy about this!" he was practically hooting.

He finally put me down and looked over at Toni and Jen, his face growing serious as he registered the fact they weren't smiling, too.

"What's up?" he asked.

"She hasn't told Dave yet," Jen said.

"She doesn't even want him to help raise the baby," Toni added.

Liam turned on me like I was insane.

"What the fuck is that all about?" he asked. "Is that true? What the hell is wrong with you?"

I sighed, having no desire to go through all this again.

"I'll let them explain it to you," I said, as I picked up my plate and walked out of the kitchen.

*

It was almost closing time and I was starving. Leaving Jen to tend the last few customers, I disappeared into the kitchen and found Liam putting away leftovers.

"Stop!" I said, racing over.

He reached behind one of the larger pots and pulled out a plate covered in foil. He handed it to me with a smile.

"Here you go, Mama," he said.

I took it gratefully, peeled back the foil, and dug in. He gently took the plate from my hands and set it on the counter before pulling out a stool for me. I climbed on and ate as he finished cleaning up.

"Shouldn't your staff be doing this?" I teased.

Liam was notorious for doing a final sweep of the kitchen before leaving for the night. He took so much pride in everything he did—even his clean-up.

"Shut up, you." He pulled out his phone and checked the screen. He grinned and shoved it back in his pocket.

"What's that all about?" I asked.

"Nothing. But it's ten to. You should go out and do last call."

I sighed and reluctantly slid off the stool, passing him my plate on the way out.

"Thanks, Chef."

"My pleasure."

I swung through the doors back into the restaurant.

"All right, last call," I bellowed.

I looked around but the restaurant was empty, save for one customer at the bar. Dave.

"Glad I made it then," he said.

I walked over to him, grabbing a few dirty glasses to deposit in the sink on the way.

"Come on, Dave. I want to go home."

"And I'd like you to make me a drink," he said.

I rolled my eyes.

"Come on. I'm tired. I don't want to play this game. You've hated every drink I ever made you."

"Wrong. I've loved every drink you've ever made me."

I stared at him, uncomprehending.

"What are you talking about?" I asked. "You—"

"Said I hated them, but I lied."

"Why would you do that?" I asked, confused.

He just smiled and reached for my hand, tracing the lines of my palm as he spoke.

"I wanted you from the first time I saw you. But I'm not an idiot. I knew you were way out of my league. I needed a way to stand out, so I went for the one place I knew I could get you— your ego."

My jaw dropped.

"You mean…"

"I mean I have loved every drink you ever made me. Each one more than the last. And I want you to make me a drink right now."

I turned, hesitant, and started mixing him a cocktail. I couldn't believe he'd gone to such lengths. I couldn't believe he'd waited this long to tell me. Why was he telling me now?

CHAPTER TWENTY-EIGHT

Dave

I watched Bree pull the bottles down from the shelf and mix my drink. I watched the way she tossed her head to get her hair out of her face, the way she shifted on one foot as she used the shaker, how she licked her lips as she poured the drink.

She set the glass down on the bar and slid it across to me. I picked it up and took a sip. Liquid heaven. I put it back down.

"There was something you wanted to talk about," I said.

She glanced around. The place was empty except for Jen at the cash and Liam hanging around by the kitchen doors.

"Nah. It's fine."

"There's nothing you want to tell me?" I asked.

She stared at me for a moment, then gave me a sad smile and shook her head.

I reached across the bar and took both her hands in mine.

"Bree. I know you're pregnant."

Her eyes flew open. She turned to Jen, then to Liam, but neither of them would meet her eye.

"Nobody told me," I said.

"Then why—?"

"You fainted at the festival. You turned green at your apartment. You threw up. You refused alcohol. You saw the doctor then told me that 'it was taken care of.' Bree, it may have taken me a while, but I'm not a complete moron."

She licked her lips nervously and I let go of her hands and got down from my stool. I walked around and went behind the bar. I didn't want anything in between us. Jen glanced over discreetly, a small smile playing at the corner of her mouth.

"Why didn't you tell me?" I whispered.

Finally, she raised her eyes to mine.

"I didn't want you to feel obligated, or tied down, or thrown into a situation you weren't ready for."

He snorted.

"Funny," he said. "And here I thought you really knew me. That's all bullshit, Bree. Why didn't you tell me?"

She closed her eyes for a long moment, and when she opened them, one plump tear fell to her cheek.

"I didn't think you'd be...prepared to take care of a baby," she whispered.

"What?"

I stepped back and looked at her, trying to wrap my head around what she was telling me. Why wouldn't I be prepared? And then it hit me. Her own upbringing. The suits. She'd been plotting a course for an easy life, and life with me wouldn't always be easy.

I took a deep breath. The last thing I wanted was to make a misstep.

"Bree, you know that I love you, right?"

She squinted.

"Do you?" she asked.

"Yes. Very much. And you know I'm perfectly capable of taking care of you and a baby."

"But this wasn't in your plan—"

"Shut up about my plan already. Don't you get it? You're my plan. You haven't derailed anything. You've created a path. You've created our future. You and me. We're going to have a baby."

Her eyes widened as if the thought occurred to her for the first time.

"You *want* to have a baby?" she asked, hesitant.

I laughed out loud and grabbed her around the waist.

"Yes. A thousand times yes. I want to have a baby with you."

"But what about the expense, and the —"

"Shhh." I put my finger to her lips. "It's never the right time and there's never enough money for a baby. My mother used to say that. And she was right, I guess. It's the kind of thing you just do. We're going to be fine, I promise. Despite the fact that I'm not a high-powered executive in a suit."

She giggled at that and I tightened the arm around her waist, pulling her closer. I kissed the top of her head.

"Now get your stuff. We're going home."

*

We walked into my house and I took Bree's bag, putting it on the hallway table. She turned to me with a hopeful look.

"Are you going to draw me a bath?" she asked, batting her eyes at me.

"No," I said.

She dropped the flirty demeanor.

"Why not?" she demanded.

"Because I haven't done the research on hot baths and early pregnancy yet. I'll make you some cocoa." I started towards the kitchen.

"Oh my god. Are you going to be one of those?" she asked.

I turned back to look at her.

"Yup."

She smiled, clearly delighted.

"I don't want cocoa. It's a million degrees out. How about some water?"

I nodded and continued to the kitchen. She kicked off her shoes and made her way to the living room, getting comfortable on the couch. I got two glasses of water and went to join her.

Putting the glasses down on the coffee table, I sank the floor at her feet. I ran my hands up her legs to her waist, then brought my left hand around and lay it flat against her belly.

"Hey, there," I whispered.

I got up on my knees and she parted her legs for me. Getting comfortable between them, I raised her tank top up over her flat belly and kissed it.

"There's nothing there yet," she said.

"Of course there is. When's the first appointment?"

"In a few weeks," she said.

"Can I come?"

"You want to come?" she asked, disbelieving.

"Bree, I want to do everything. I also think you should stay here."

She removed my hands, which had been fondling her belly, and leaned forward to look me in the eye.

"Dave. We've been dating for a minute. Please tell me you didn't just ask me to move in with you."

"I didn't. I'm just asking you to stay for a bit."

She eyed me suspiciously.

"How long?"

"I don't know. Maybe until the baby is eighteen or so?"

She burst out laughing.

"Look," I pleaded. "We'll take it one day at a time. I just want to make sure you're okay. That the two of you have everything you need. I understand we're at the start of our relationship, but we're also having a baby. Both those things are happening at the same time. We need to figure out how to navigate that."

She looked at me, then down at her belly, a slow smile spreading across her face.

"Let me think about it," she said.

"Deal," I said. "Now take off your pants."

She blinked once, then stood up and obeyed.

"You have plans?" she asked, stepping out of her jeans and tossing them aside.

"Tank top, too."

She rolled her eyes and pulled off her top. I circled my finger at her, indicating the bra should come off, too. She reached behind her to unclasp it, then stopped and narrowed her eyes at me.

"You take off stuff, too," she said. "Starting with your shirt, please."

I stood up and grinned, pulling my shirt over my head. She walked over and placed her palms flat against my chest, her eyes fluttering. It sent a shot right down to my groin—both her touch and seeing the effect I had on her.

With one hand, she reached around again and unhooked her bra, then peeled it off and tossed it in the corner. She took a step towards me, gazing up into my eyes as she pressed her chest against mine. I felt her nipples harden against me and my dick responded in kind.

"Is it true?" I asked, my voice suddenly husky. "About pregnant women being horny?"

"So fucking true," she growled as she tore at my jeans.

I laughed and reached down to help her. She dropped to her knees and as I peeled my boxer briefs down, she took me in hand, leaned forward, and licked the tip. My knees buckled and I reached behind to ease myself down on the couch. She spread my thighs, and looking straight up at me, took my entire length into her mouth.

"Oh, *fuck.*"

She moaned in agreement, one hand on my thigh, the other squeezing the base of my cock. Fire rushed through my veins as her tongue worked its magic on me. She'd take me right to the edge, then back off, as if she never wanted me to come. Knowing how much it turned her on drove me nuts, and at that moment her hand moved down between her thighs.

"Bree," I choked. "You're killing me."

She gave me an evil grin, then slowly re-leased me from her mouth. She climbed up into my lap and lowered herself onto me, guiding my still rock-hard cock inside. We both made a couple of indecipherable noises as she started moving. I reached for her tits, leaning forward to take one nipple in my mouth. She cried out and I smiled against her, already enjoying the increased sensitivity of her pregnancy.

"Touch me," she said, stalling me by making slow circles with her hips.

She pulled my head away from her breast and looked at me with pleading eyes. I leaned back against the couch, putting my hands on her hips.

"Touch yourself," I said quietly.

She closed her eyes and reached down to where we were joined. She rubbed along my length as she rose slowly, then thrust back down against me. Her hand moved up towards her clit, and as she found a rhythm with me, her thumb found a rhythm with herself. Her nipples were rock hard and I reached up to pinch one lightly.

"Open your eyes," I said firmly.

Her eyes flew open and she stared at me, her entire face awash in desire. She looked so incredibly sexy that I grabbed hold of her hips and thrust into her as I came. She let out a cry as she followed, grasping my shoulders and digging her fingernails into my back as we rode out our orgasms together. Her head dropped onto my shoulder and my arms went around her.

"I love you, too," she whispered into my ear.

"Nice to hear you finally say it."

*

I woke up the next morning with a smile on my face and only one thing on my mind. It was

Sunday. The shop was closed and Bree didn't have to be at work until five. I rolled over and reached for her, my dick already twitching in anticipation.

But she wasn't there. I felt around before lifting my head for visual evidence. Her clothes were still on the chair in the corner, so she hadn't left. I sat up and looked around. Then I heard it.

I leapt out of bed and made my way to the bathroom down the hall, as the unmistakable sounds of retching got increasingly louder. I knocked on the door.

"Bree?"

I heard her clear her throat.

"Uh, yeah?"

"You okay?"

"Uh, well, I am throwing up."

"Yeah, I hear that. Is there anything I can do?"

There was a pause as she retched into the toilet again.

"Uh, I don't think so. I'm just gonna stay here and do this for a few more hours. That okay?"

I stood there, blinking. How the fuck should I know if that was okay?

"I don't know. Is that okay? Should you be this sick?"

She laughed, which brought on another bout of retching.

"This happens every morning," she said weakly.

"Okay. That's it. You're staying with me."

CHAPTER TWENTY-NINE

Epilogue

"Bree?"

"Yeah?"

"I don't know how to tell you this, but I'm thinking maybe it's time to call it on work?"

I lifted my head from behind the bar to stare at Adam. It was the end of another busy night and the last customers were just leaving the restaurant. I dropped a dishrag and I'd been trying to retrieve it, but it took me a while to get back into a standing position.

"What's that supposed to mean?" I asked.

Liam and Toni came out from the kitchen and walked over to join Adam, while Jen walked over from the hostess stand and took her place by me. I looked at each of them in turn, my eyes narrow and suspicious.

"What's going on here?" I asked. "Somebody talk to me."

Jen reached over and put her hand on my shoulder. I turned to her.

"Sweetie, you're eight months pregnant. You're bigger than a house. The customers are finding it weird to buy drinks from you."

I looked down at my belly. So maybe it was a little big, but a house?

"You think I look like a house?"

Jen sighed and shook her head.

"Listen, Bree," Adam said. "We tried to be gentle. We tried to be subtle. The only reason you're still working is because it's off-season and there are no tourists to see an eight-month pregnant woman mixing cocktails. Go home. Have a baby. Then get the hell back here."

I looked over at Liam and he nodded. Toni cocked her head and gave me a sympathetic smile.

"I guess I am kind of tired," I said.

A collective sigh of relief rose up from the group.

"And my ankles are killing me," I continued.

"Dave called twenty minutes ago. He's on his way to pick you up."

I blushed. I'd had to stop driving three weeks prior when I could no longer fit behind the wheel. I grabbed my bag and walked out from behind the bar. One by one, they each came over to hug me.

"Come on, guys, I'm still going to see you all the time," I said as a traitorous tear slipped down my cheek.

Liam reached over and wiped it away, taking my face in his hands.

"I'll bring you food all the time. I promise."

"I'll hold you to that," I said, smiling.

I gave Adam a final squeeze and walked towards the door. When I exited the restaurant, I saw Dave standing outside in the parking lot, leaning up against his car. He was dressed in a dark suit and a crisp white shirt, no tie. His hair was pulled back. I was so stunned, I stumbled. He raced forward to catch my elbow, steadying me.

"Hey," he said.

"Hey," I whispered. "What's going on?"

He looked puzzled, and I looked down at his clothes. His eyes followed my gaze and a look of understanding came over him.

"I had a dinner meeting in Rocky Heights," he said.

Rocky Heights was the resort town about half an hour away. Dave rarely left Mountain Valley, so it must have been something important. I waited.

"Isabelle and I closed a deal on a second location," he said, grinning.

"What? Are you serious?" I asked, in a state of complete disbelief.

"Dead serious. It's a smaller location, but there are ten times the tourists and they're in a much higher income bracket. It's a win/win situation."

"Holy shit," I said. "You are a businessman."

He just shrugged and gave me a mysterious smile.

"Though I think I prefer you in the jeans and concert shirts," I added, a smile in my voice.

I slid into the car and after shutting my door, he went around to the driver's side and got in. We pulled out onto the road and he reached for the radio. I put out my hand to stop him.

"Congratulations, Dave. You should be really proud."

A smile lit up his face and he turned to me, his eyes full of love.

"How was your night?" he asked.

I felt my entire body deflate like a popped balloon.

"They kicked me out," I said, resigned.

"I'm sorry," he said. "But maybe it's not such a bad idea. You've only got a few more weeks. You should enjoy them."

I shrugged.

"How will they manage?" he asked.

"Jen will take over the bar and they'll hire a hostess for the next year. They'll hold the job for me."

"They'd be crazy not to," he said, reaching over to squeeze my hand.

We pulled up to the house and Dave parked the car. As we walked through the front door, I kicked off my shoes, relieved to be home. I'd given in right away, that very first morning, and he'd spent his entire day off moving my essentials from my place to his. I hadn't looked back since.

Things between us were amazing. I had never been with someone before who not only tolerated the real me but craved it. He'd settle for nothing less. And I felt the same way about him. I loved everything about him, and I laughed at myself for spending so many years chasing something that never could've made me happy.

For four months, he held my hair every morning as I threw up. As the pregnancy progressed, he indulged in every whim and craving I had. If I got up in the middle of the night for a sandwich, he'd look at me and say, "I could use a sandwich," and stumble out of bed right along with me.

He came to every doctor's appointment, every test, every ultrasound. He tracked the development of our baby religiously. He checked every dish Liam brought into the house before letting me eat it. He drove me crazy. I loved him for it.

I turned towards the bedroom but he took my hand and pulled me towards him. I smiled sleepily and got closer, wrapping my arms around him and landing a soft kiss on his lips.

"Come with me," he whispered. "I want to show you something."

He took my hand and walked me two rooms down the hall. The house was larger than two people required, and there were a couple of rooms we never bothered with. I tended to keep the doors closed so I wouldn't feel guilty about not cleaning them, so I was curious and maybe a little nervous to see what he wanted to 'show me.' Surely he wasn't about to hold me responsible for a lack of dusting when I was eight months pregnant with his child.

He opened the door and stepped in, beckoning me to follow as he turned on the light. The room was painted in white and the palest yellow, with a swarm of painted balloons in the corner, reaching for the ceiling. There was a solid oak crib, clearly made by Logan, and a matching changing table. A few stuffed animals lined a small shelf on the opposite wall and a mobile hung directly over the crib. It was perfect.

I turned to look at him, wonder in my eyes.

"When did you do this?" I asked.

"While you've been at work for the past six months."

I bit my lip.

"I haven't opened this door in six months?" I asked.

He burst out laughing.

"Do you like it?" he asked.

I studied the room, then looked at him.

"Are you trying to get me to stay once the baby's born?" I asked.

He reached over and skimmed his thumb across my breast.

"I've been trying to do that since the day you moved in," he murmured.

I walked around, touching everything, running my hand along the beautifully carved wood. I turned to him.

"I love it," I said.

A smile bloomed across his face, but he didn't make a move towards me. I rolled my eyes and grinned sheepishly.

"Fine. And I'll stay."

He crossed the room in two strides and tried to sweep me up in his arms, but failed miserably. We both laughed as we almost tumbled to the ground. Thankfully, the dresser was solid. He righted both of us, then took my face in his hands, leaning in and kissing me gently.

"Are you trying to seduce me, Mr. Winter?" I asked slyly.

"Damn straight I am," he mumbled. "Think you can still manage it?"

I put my hands on his shoulders, leaning up to return the kiss.

"Only one way to find out," I said.